The Front Porch Bunch

To: Kamryn

Mark R. Duffey 07

The Front Porch Bunch

Mary R. Duffey

Bloomington, IN      Milton Keynes, UK

authorHOUSE®

AuthorHouse™
1663 Liberty Drive, Suite 200
Bloomington, IN 47403
www.authorhouse.com
Phone: 1-800-839-8640

AuthorHouse™ UK Ltd.
500 Avebury Boulevard
Central Milton Keynes, MK9 2BE
www.authorhouse.co.uk
Phone: 08001974150

First published by AuthorHouse 1/17/2007

ISBN: 978-1-4259-6379-8 (sc)

Library of Congress Control Number: 2006909012

Printed in the United States of America
Bloomington, Indiana

This book is printed on acid-free paper.

*This book is dedicated to Elizabeth and Laura
and to children everywhere
who love dogs and a good story.*

Part One ❖

~ Free To Explore ~

It was a cool day in late September. The sun was shining through wispy white clouds. The laundry was already hanging on the clothesline in the back yard. Kate had been up and working since seven-thirty.

Mike had made a short run to Jake's Feed Store in Jersey County. He had unloaded the three sacks of feed by ten and was looking forward to some breakfast.

The four smaller dogs were on the big front porch—Holly, Cap, and Lass—Kate's three Scottish Terriers—and Angus—the terrier-mix who had come to live with them not so long ago.

The old porch, with its high rails and portable gate, confined the dogs, but kept them safe.

Holly was half-awake, resting comfortably on the fleece blanket that Kate had made for her. Her whiskers waved in the gentle breeze. Her right ear twitched with each new sound that came from inside the house.

She heard the rustle of the morning paper and the tinkle of coffee cups on saucers. Holly knew that Kate and Mike were having their second cup of coffee of the morning. She also knew that Mike had just eaten another biscuit—with strawberry jelly.

Oh! How Holly loved strawberry jelly! In fact, she had watched Kate preserve jar after jar just last Spring. She remembered how Kate would give her a taste every now and again, right from her finger.

Cap was peering out at his front yard through his wooden porch rail. He was wondering if an animal, an animal of any kind, was going to invade his yard.

Lass was licking her paws with her long, pink tongue. Her small brown eyes sparkled as she licked. She was the most beautiful dog on the farm and she took her grooming quite seriously.

A fly buzzed by Cap's ear. He snapped at it. "'Missed him," he muttered to himself. "But he won't be ar-rr-round much longer-rr! The next time he comes by, I'll nab him! That's a sur-rr-re thing!" he muttered again.

Angus, however, was the busiest of the four. He paid no attention to what the others were doing. He was always headed for somewhere or something. He rambled and roamed from one porch corner to the next, his toenails scratching on the slick wooden floor, in search of anything he could find.

He loved the clumps of dust that rolled into balls when he pushed them with his nose. He loved to see tiny spiders scurry away as he tried to get a good look at them. Angus liked to watch the tall grass wave in the breeze and smell the purple Iris that grew along the east end of the porch in the Spring. He liked hearing the boards creak as he ran across them. The two loose ones in front of the porch steps made the best sound of all.

Cap and Holly just let him be. They loved their newest, littlest friend. They understood that he was *curious*, as all young pups are.

Lass? She was different. Lass had no real opinion when it came to Angus. She thought only of the important things in life—her diet and her grooming.

Mike gave Kate's dogs plenty of attention, to be sure, but he especially enjoyed watching Kate with them.

She would pet them, play with them, bathe them, comb them, feed them, hug them, squeeze them, and even kiss them. Sometimes she'd make special bows for Lass' ears and soft collar covers for Holly and Cap. Mike also noticed how Kate would make sure that Angus had more than enough food in his dish at suppertime.

Holly had been a very special gift to Kate from her father. The cream-colored wheaten puppy had arrived several Christmases ago. She was adorned with a sprig of holly attached to a red ribbon collar. Holly was the nicest gift that Kate had ever received—in all her Christmases!

Cap, the dark, brindled Scottie, was the puppy that Kate chose from a litter of four as a playmate for Holly.

Kate's eyes twinkled when she first saw him. He was the most darling puppy—chewing on a blue denim cap in the corner of his bed.

Kate still had that cap. It was in a small box on the top shelf of her sewing room closet—right next to the sprig of artificial holly and short length of red ribbon.

Lass *was* the most beautiful dog on the farm, if you were to ask her, because Katie had said so.

5

It was just two years ago that she had heard Katie tell Mike, "Oh! What a beautiful, *beautiful* little *lass*! Why! I never expected *anything as lovely as this*! Look at those *eyes* — like shiny *buttons*, they are! And her *coat*! It's as black as *night*! Thank you! *Thank you, Mike*! What a *lovely* anniversary gift! She's perfect, just *perfect*!"

Angus' story is one of a different kind.

Mike was driving to Lewiston when he first saw the lost pup near the chain-link fence by the quarry.

Mike looked at his tag. He hoped to see a name, an address, an inscription of any kind that would help him find the pup's rightful owners — but there was none.

Of course, he had taken him home to Kate.

"Is he part Scottie?" Mike had asked her.

No. He had *some* terrier in him though, and was part something else, she had guessed.

(Mike had laughed and said that he was "something else", alright!)

Of course, the puppy needed a name of some sort, at least for the time being, until his owners came for him. Kate chose "Angus" — the name that would *make* him Scottish.

They placed an ad in the local newspaper and posted "LOST PUPPY" pictures at the animal clinic, library, grocery store, coffee shop, and hair salon.

A week went by.

No luck.

Three weeks went by.

Still, no luck.

Kate gave little Angus lots of extra attention and the best of care.

She tried not to get too attached to him, but that was impossible. The pup followed her everywhere. He nosed his way into her chair, under her sofa pillow, and into her heart. She loved him already.

It wasn't long until the once scrawny, scraggly little dog had gained some good weight, and had settled in nicely with the others.

Cap and Holly enjoyed watching him play. Sometimes he made them laugh right out loud.

Holly marveled at how quickly he had learned their household routine, and Cap liked the way the young one had treated Holly from the very beginning — always remembering to say "Yes, Ma'am" and "Excuse me." There was no doubt about it. They liked him just fine.

Mike finally spoke to Kate about him. He wondered if she would like to keep him after all.

Kate hugged Mike so tight, right then and there, that she had nearly thrown him off balance!

Angus received his round of shots and license the very next week.

Now, Holly, Cap, Lass, and Angus were not the *only* dogs on Mike and Kate's farm. One other dog lived there too. Ellie, the Airedale, was the dog that *Mike* knew and loved best.

Ellie was a hard-working, yet gentle dog, with a kind spirit.

The tall, muscular, wooly-coated dog was too large for the breed, but as far as Mike was concerned, her large size made it all the better for taking care of things around the place. After all, she was not a show dog or a breeding dog. She was his *working dog* — the dog that guarded Kate and the farm.

It was on the eleventh of March, just two days after Mike's birthday, that he had driven to Brad's place to get her—the dog that Brad could no longer keep.

"If things don't work out, I'll bring her back and help you find a good home for her," Mike had told him, but Ellie took to country life in no time!

It wasn't long until Mike knew that Ellie was going to be the kind of farm dog he'd hoped she'd be.

Ellie was lying in her favorite place, this particular Saturday morning, in the way that she always did. She was lying on her right side in the cool dirt that she had just scratched up from under the picnic table. A small tire, with a long rope looped through it, lay next to her.

More often than not, where Ellie was, so was the tire. It was her favorite possession. It was the toy that Mike had made for her.

Mike stood on the porch and looked over the farm. It was a beautiful morning. The air was clean and fresh. It was a bit cool, but that was the kind of weather Mike preferred.

Angus yipped at him, begging for a treat.

"No. It's not dinner time yet, fella! You're gonna have to wait quite for a while for *that*, I'm afraid," he said, grinning. He tousled the pup's whiskers and returned to the kitchen.

He picked up the notepad that lay on the telephone table in the corner. He flipped three pages over and read the number. He dialed it.

"Good morning, Matt! You're just the guy I need to speak to! This is Mike. Did you remember about today? Yeah. Kate and I are goin' into town and the horses will be needin' to be let out at around three or so. Yep. And I'll check the outer gate before I leave. I'll catch up with you on it tomorrow. We'll be back by five. Yep. I'll take it from there. Thanks a lot, Matt. You bet. 'Bye."

Kate was finishing up the last few dishes. Her shopping list lay on the table.

Mike gave her a kiss on the cheek and told her he'd be back in just a bit. He wanted to check on things before they left for town. He wondered if she'd be ready. She said that she would.

Kate walked to the pantry to see if they had enough cinnamon. She had been meaning to buy more of that for a while. She also wondered about baking soda. She shook the box. Yes, she needed that too.

Ellie heard Mike come out of the back door and immediately joined him in the middle of the yard.

"Let's go, Girl," Mike said, giving her a scratch behind her right ear.

Ellie trotted along at Mike's left side, staying close to him every step of the way. Her long tan legs were supported by large furry feet, yet she was surprisingly graceful.

Doing farm rounds was easy for Ellie now. She knew exactly where they were going. They would go to the pasture first, bring in the horses, and then make a quick check of the pasture gate. Next stop, the chicken coop, and finally, her favorite place of all, the work shed.

Mike gave a loud whistle and then a holler. "Rex! Judy! Come on! Let's go!" He clicked his tongue. "C'mon! 'Gotta get in now!"

Judy trotted to the fence, followed by Rex.

Ellie sat, watching the big animals.

Mike took sugar cubes from his shirt pocket and gave each of them two.

Rex nuzzled his pocket for more.

"Nope. That's all, buddy. No more. Gotta go in for now," Mike said to the horse as he took hold of his halter. He unlatched the gate. He led the horse to the left and told Judy, "Stay back!" He closed the gate and led Rex into the barn.

Judy neighed, but Ellie paid little attention. Instead, she was focused upon the sounds coming from inside the barn.

Mike whistled as he went about the business of feeding and watering.

He returned for Judy.

Judy whinnied softly and rubbed her soft nose against Mike's shoulder. He patted her. "You're a good girl," he said as he took her halter into his large fingers and unlatched the gate once more.

Judy followed him obediently into her stall. "Matt will be here later on to let you out. Behave, now," he said, closing her gate.

Judy neighed softly.

Mike met Ellie outside. "Let's go," he said.

They walked to the pasture. Mike checked the gate. It was secure.

He didn't like the idea of his horses being out to pasture for the day without his being there to check on them every now and then. Too many things could happen. He'd seen horses get into trouble before, real bad trouble, with no one around. He sure didn't want that to happen at his place.

Young Matt Johnson would be by, for sure, at three. He was a good kid—responsible, reliable. He was used to being around horses and was serious about his chores. Mike also knew that Matt appreciated the extra spending money he earned helping out.

Mike and Ellie walked toward the chicken coop.

The big dog stayed calm in the midst of all the clucking and flapping. She sat.

Ellie watched as Mike scooped yellow corn from an aluminum pail and scattered it on the ground. He drew fresh water into the old dish pan and placed it in the shade of the coop.

Ellie knew that their next stop would be at the shed. She looked at Mike eagerly. She wanted to bark, but she knew better than to do that. She knew it would upset the hens. Instead, she whined softly.

Mike smiled. He knew what she wanted. "Yeah. It's time. Let's get on to the shed, Girl. We're finished here."

Ellie wagged her tail. She joined Mike at his left side. They began walking. Mike whistled part of an old tune that Ellie had heard many times before.

The path felt soft under Ellie's feet. The gentle breeze waved through her wooly coat. She searched for crickets and dragonflies, but her mind was on something else, something much more important.

Mike stopped whistling as they neared the work shed. He took the key from his pocket and unlocked the door.

Ellie looked to see if her basketball was still on her rug.

It was!

The ball was flat from many hours of play but she still treasured it.

The latest issue of Mike's favorite fishing magazine lay on the rickety table. It invited him to read, but he thought better of it. He knew that Kate was waiting for him.

Ellie picked up the ball. She wagged her tail and looked at him with pleading eyes.

Mike knew what she wanted but he pretended not to know. This was all part of the game.

She pranced.

He looked away.

She whined.

Mike still ignored her.

Ellie woofed and nudged him with her nose.

Mike grinned as he peeked at the big dog.

She stood very still now, begging for just *one throw*!

Mike snatched the limp ball. He tossed it out the door, into the air!

Ellie was off like a shot!

The ball landed near the Snowball Bush. Ellie wrapped her large mouth around it and carried it back to him.

"Drop it!" Mike commanded.

She dropped the ball at his feet.

He picked it up and spun around. The big dog's heart was pounding with excitement as she reared, waiting for him to throw it again.

He threw it once more.

The agile dog leaped and caught it in a mid-air spring!

"Good girl!" Mike shouted.

Ellie dropped the ball at his feet.

"Okay! One more time, and that's *it*! We gotta get back to the house!" Mike threw the ball with all his might this time.

Ellie ran like the wind to retrieve it! She snorted triumphantly as she carried it back.

Mike took it from her. "That's all, Girl. We gotta get goin'! Kate's waitin' on us." He stepped inside the door and dropped the ball on her rug.

Ellie hung her head. She knew the game was over.

He patted her shoulder. "We'll play some more this evening. I promise, Girl. C'mon! We better get back. It's gettin' late."

Ellie joined him at his left side. She wagged her tail, knowing that his kind words were just for her.

The clouds had cleared. The sun shone brilliantly as they walked toward the house.

Mike put the big ice chest in the back of his new '86 pick-up. He needed it to hold the cold grocery items they would buy in town.

Ellie cocked her head. She watched. She felt anxious. She knew that Mike and Kate would be leaving soon.

He tossed her an ice cube. She crushed it in an instant and swallowed. He tossed her another. She crushed it too, with her huge teeth. She waited for more, but Mike closed the lid to the chest.

Ellie let out one resounding bark. She wagged her tail, but she already knew the answer.

"*No,* Girl. Not *this* trip," Mike said softly to her. He rubbed her neck. "We'll be back pretty soon. We won't be gone long."

Kate had tidied up in the kitchen. The laundry was not quite dry on the line, so that would have to wait until she returned.

She had checked on her "loves", as she called them, and made sure that the porch gate was in place.

"Are you ready to go, hon?" Mike asked as he came into the kitchen.

Kate put her jacket on and picked up her purse from the kitchen table. "I'm ready," she said. "Mike, would you grab that pillow for me? I need to match up some fabric with it today. 'Gonna make new curtains for the spare room."

"Sure," Mike said, as he took the small pillow from the counter top. They walked toward the back door. "'You need anything else?"

"No. I think that's it," she said.

Mike locked the door.

Ellie followed them from the back porch to the edge of the yard.

Kate patted the dog's head. "We've got to go to town today, Girl. We'll be back."

"Keep an eye on things, Ellie!" Mike said.

Ellie sat as Mike started down the dirt lane. She watched from the edge of the yard until the truck disappeared from sight.

She walked to the back porch and sat near the top step. She knew that she was in charge now.

Lucy jumped from the barn ladder to the dirt floor.

She was no longer the beautiful cat that she once was. Her long gray and white fur was matted in places and her left ear was missing a small piece at its tip. Her teeth were yellowed, but they were still sharp and needle-like. She prided herself in still being a good mouser.

She had lived in the barn on that farm for many years now, and called its back left corner her home.

With no litters of kittens to care for any longer, she spent most of her days there, sheltered from winter's cold and summer's heat.

She had plenty to eat, with all the mice in, and around the barn. Sometimes too, The Lady would bring her warm milk and cornbread in a dish from the kitchen, or scraps of meat from their dinner plates. Lucy also knew where The Man put the fish bones after cleaning his catch from the pond.

Lucy liked Judy and Rex well enough. They had decided to tolerate each other years ago. Still, the cat knew to keep a watchful eye on them. She knew the horses could kick, if they wanted to.

More often than not, the cat preferred staying there, in the barn, in her corner, lounging the day away—

But every once in a while, it was fun to go creeping along the front of the house, near, but not too close to, that old porch.

The four littler dogs with long whiskers and big ears barked and lunged at her every time they saw her!

She thrived on her taunting and teasing of them. Lucy loved to *meow at them* and *hiss at them* and *spit at them* from the edge of the front yard. She delighted in *sneering at them* with her jagged teeth showing.

And, Cap! Oh, that *Cap*! He was the worst of all! What a conceited, self-centered little *cur*! How Lucy loved twitching her long gray tail at *him* any chance she had! (Didn't he know that *she too*, could scratch and bite?)

Of course, the big Airedale was never a problem. That dog had been trained well and knew not to chase *any* of the animals on that farm—not even *her*. The Man had seen to that.

Angus sat, panting on the porch near Cap. Cap ignored the sound his panting made. He was hoping to spy a butterfly or a grasshopper, or even another fly.

Holly slept quietly in her spot by the wicker chair as Lass looked toward the front door, wondering why it was so quiet inside the house.

"'Wonder how long we're going to have to stay here!" Angus said. "I'm tired of this old porch! There's nothin' to do!" He cocked his head. "Aren't you *bored*, Cap? Don't ya ever want to just run and run and *explore stuff? Huh?*"

Cap didn't answer.

"*Cap?*"

Cap looked directly at Little Angus. He squared his shoulders and gave the order. "Ssshh! Don't wor-r-rry aboot it! They'll be back! Why don't yoo take a snooze or-rr something?"

"In the middle of the *morning*?" Angus screeched.

"Well, then find something tooo doo, and stop all that *br-r-reathing*! I'm busy herr-r-e, Ang-gie! I'm lookin' for-r a hor-rrsefly! Can't yoo see that?"

Angus scowled. He hated being called "Ang-gie".

Cap continued searching.

The pup sat down by Lass, but she did not notice. She was too busy with her grooming. She was also wondering what she'd have in her dinner dish tonight. She hoped there would be chicken or lean beef in her meal. What's more, she even enjoyed the bites of lettuce Kate would sometimes add to her supper. She thought that any bit of salad was a very special treat. She liked the crispness of the leaves as she chewed, and liked the taste of the light, creamy dressing that clung to the side of her dish.

Angus stretched onto the smooth floor. He sighed.

Cap, annoyed with the lot of them, walked to the other end of the porch.

Angus laid his chin on his front paws. He closed his eyes and tried to rest, but his mind was just too busy with thoughts of dust balls, and spiders, of new smells, and sights to see.

Holly looked around from where she lay and closed her eyes once more.

She was soon off again in a place all her own. She dreamed of walks with Kate, and of bites of soft, moist banana bread.

Suddenly, the pup sat up. "Let's play a *game*!" he shouted. "*Lass! You're* **IT!**"

"Angus! *No-o!*" she groaned. "I *do* need to finish my grooming. I just don't *feel* like it! Maybe *Cap* or *Holly* will play."

Angus looked hopefully at Holly, but she was sleeping.

He glanced at Cap, but Cap was leaning on the porch rail with his front paws, eyeing a ladybug that had landed nearby.

Angus asked anyway. "'Wanna *play*, Cap?"

"Nope."

"'Ya *sure*?"

Cap's brows moved forward as he looked head-on at Angus. "'Can't! 'Busy! I alrr-r-ready told yoo that! Didn't yoo listen tooo me the *fir-r-st time*, young'in?"

Cap didn't want to be so hard on Angus, but even *young'ins* had to learn not to be so interruptive when grown-ups were busy. He lowered his tail and made the motion for Angus to lie down.

Angus yipped playfully, hoping to coax Cap into changing his mind, but Cap looked at him sternly.

The pup knew that Cap was not to be pushed too far.

Mike and Kate were almost to town.

The gardening show would be on in just a few minutes. Kate liked listening to that program. She learned quite a lot from it. She especially liked hearing about new home remedies for insects and weeds in her garden.

Mike didn't care much about what they listened to. He was glad to just settle back and do the driving.

Cattails swayed, as frogs and bugs jumped and buzzed all along the pond's edge. Fish jumped occasionally too, as the tall grasses waved in the breeze. The noon-day sun was mirrored on the face of the pond.

Ellie moved carefully through the grass, her nose to the ground, searching for anything out of the ordinary.

Finally deciding that things were in order, she made her way up the slope toward the sweet smell of the dirt lane that ran along the front of the house.

"Oh, my goodness! I've slept past *noon!*" Holly said to herself as she sat up with a start.

Angus jumped to his feet. "What's wrong, Ma'am?" he asked.

"Nothing, Angus. Why, nothing *at all,*" she replied. "I didn't mean to *frighten* you."

Angus stretched, and then seated himself next to her.

Holly smiled at him.

"Holly, I wanna *ask* you something."

"Yes, Dear?"

"Holly, have you ever been exploring on your own?"

"What do you mean, Dear?" she asked.

"I mean, all by yourself?"

"Well, I used to go for long walks with Mimi in the city." (Holly often called Kate "Mimi". After all, Kate *was* her *mother,* and besides, she liked the *sound* of it.) "And, when we came here, Mimi still took me on a leash all around the farm, and even into the barn."

"No. I mean *awll by yourself.* You know, *without* Katie or Mike?"

"Why do you *ask,* Dear?"

"Because I've never been past the *yard,* except *to* the *barn,* and that was only *once.* Why, I'll bet there's a big, gigantic *world* out there to see! 'Millions of things! Well, I *think so*, anyway."

"Angus?"

"Yes, Ma'am?"

"Do you remember that you *have* been exploring before — before Mike found you? You were out there — all by yourself. You had no one — and you were *alone*?"

"Yeah. I *remember*," Angus replied.

"Well then, you *have* had a chance to explore before, Angus. 'Right?"

"Ma'am?" Angus said.

"Yes?"

"Pardon me for saying this, but that was *not exploring*. That was *not* having *fun*. My old fam'ly didn't *watch me* careful enough! I shoulda stayed in the car! I just looked over — and they were *gone*! They *drived away*!"

Holly licked his face gently with her tongue. "Now, *now*, Dear."

"I tried to *tell* them, but they couldn't *hear* me!"

"Oh, Angus. Don't you worry about that, Dear. It's just one of those things that we call an *unfortunate incident*. No one *meant* for you to be separated from your other family. *You* didn't want that, and *they* didn't want that either. Do you *understand that*, Angus?"

He sniffled. "I think so, Holly. I *think* I do," he said.

She nudged him gently. "Well, *anyway*. You're *here*, Angus — and, we *love* you. That's all that matters now." She looked around the big porch. "Why, this is a *fine* place! We're all here — *together*! *We're* a family now."

"Holly?"

"*Hmm*?"

"Would *you* like to go exploring with me? We wouldn't have to go *far*. Just around out there a little ways? *Huh*?"

"Oh, *no* Dear! We mus'n't *ever* do that!"

19

"Why *not?*"

Holly started to speak, but Angus interrupted her. "*Cap* wants to—*all the time!* And, *Ellie?* *She* explores every day, Ma'am! Every *day!*"

"Angus, I'm too *old* now, and there are *dangers* out there. *Truly*, there are! And, as for *Cap?* He's been *scolded* for going too far!"

Angus sighed.

"*Ellie?* She goes places because that's her job."

"What do you mean, Ma'am?"

"Well, a *job*, Angus! *You* know. That's when you have places to *be*, and things to *do*, because you're *supposed* to. Like, Ellie makes sure that our farm is *safe*. She checks on things all through*out* the day. Do you understand? And Mike and Mimi *count on her* to take care of things while they are away."

"Oh," replied Angus. "Well, *I* could help take care of things *too!*"

"No, Angus. You're too young. And, we're not big dogs like *she* is."

"Well, we're still *tough!* Look at *Cap!* He's *really* tough!"

"Well, yes, maybe so. But not like *Ellie*. She can *run* and *hunt* and *fight*, Angus. My! She could bite us into *pieces* if she wanted to! You see, Angus, we're Mimi's *pets*. We're not *hunting dogs*, or *working dogs* — but Ellie *is*."

Angus looked at the floor. He guessed he understood. But, oh! How lonely it was sometimes on that porch!

If he could — if he could only —

His thoughts trailed off into a daydream of rocks and hills — of trees and ponds — of creeks — and blue skies.

Lass jumped onto the silver milk crate that Mike had turned upside-down to use as a foot stool. She rolled her eyes around at Cap who was snoring at his end of the porch. How ridiculous he sounded — making all that noise!

Kate and Mike parked next to the small grocery store that had the good variety of flavored teas. Mike helped Kate out of the truck and locked the door.

Kate's first thoughts were of getting the groceries they needed. She knew that she wanted to get the cold meats packed in ice as soon as possible.

She was hoping to be back no later than five, but she'd just have to see how things went. The list was a long one.

"He sure is a *skinny little thing*," Lucy thought to herself as she watched Angus from under the porch steps. She knew that the little dog could not see her, and she took pride in the fact that she was fooling him.

Holly had strolled to the far end of the porch. She hoped that there would be delicious leftovers in her dinner tonight.

Lucy heard the big curly dog coming alongside the house. She sprang to her feet and ducked under the porch. Her long white whiskers brushed against the support post as she listened.

"Hi, everybody!" Ellie said.

Cap sat up, greeting her along with the others.

"Hi, Ellie!"

"Hello ther-rr-e!"

"What's goin' on?"

"'Nice to see you!"

"'Just checkin' things out, and thought I'd say Hullo," Ellie said with a big smile. "'Not much happenin' though. Whut you kids up to?"

"Nothin'. Nothin' at *all!*" Angus reported.

"'Just resting here while Mimi and Mike are gone," Holly said.

"Yuh," Ellie said, yawning.

"Would yoo like tooo join us?" Cap asked.

"Uh, no thanks," she said. "I'm gonna go round back. 'Got tuh keep a eye on things. If yuh need anything, just give a holler, okay?"

"Okay," Holly said.

"'See yoo later-r-r, Ellie," Cap said.

They watched as the big dog disappeared from sight.

Lass licked her whiskers, smoothing them into place.

Lucy sprang toward the barn.

Cap lunged forward and stood on his hind legs. He braced himself with his front paws against the porch rail. His nose twitched fiercely. His keen brown eyes were sighted on her as she grew smaller and smaller in the distance. "That *cat!*" he muttered to himself. "I have *no use* for-rr-r her-rr!"

He turned to the others. "Anyone know when Katie and Mike will be back? I'm gettin' a wee bit hungrr-r-ry! A bite would doo just fine aboot now!"

"You're *always* hungry, Cap! It isn't even *close* to dinner time," Lass scoffed.

"'Any chew bones lyin' 'r-r-rround?" he asked again, ignoring her.

"Yeah. By the water bowls," Angus said.

Cap chose the biggest one and began gnawing. He worked his teeth into every twist and fold of the rawhide.

Lass returned to her grooming as Holly dozed at the far end of the porch again.

The half-grown pup lay on his side. His ribs and belly moved evenly with every breath he took. He looked at the grain of the wood floor, smelled the familiar smell of rawhide, and wondered if he'd ever have a *real* adventure.

The groceries were already in the truck and the cold foods were in the ice chest.

Mike walked to Bert's Hardware Store while Kate looked at fabrics just a few doors down.

Kate McKinney had it narrowed down to three prints before she knew it.

She walked out onto the sidewalk and looked up and down the street. People were strolling by with their treasures of the day.

"Hi, Hon. Are you finished with your shopping?" Mike asked.

"Oh! Hi! Yeah. I'm finished," she said.

"How about some lunch?" Mike suggested.

"'Lunch Room?" she wanted to know.

"Yeah, that's what *I* was thinking," he said.

Kate smiled. She especially liked their chicken salad sandwiches with the large Bread and Butter pickle slices.

Mike put the fabric in the truck behind the back of her seat and helped her in. He wondered what the Special of the Day was.

It wasn't much past two when Ellie was stirred from her sleep. "What in the world is goin' *on*?" she wondered as she jumped to her feet.

She listened. The squawking, almost screaming-like sounds, were coming from the coop!

The big black and tan dog's body was swift and sure! She ran through the weeds and wildflowers along the narrow path

23

that led to the chicken house. With her nose in the air, and her eyes as wide as silver dollars, she raced!

As she neared the coop, she slowed her run to a walk.

As quiet as any dog could possibly be, is exactly what she was. Ellie crept toward the small opening in the east side of the coop. She put her paws upon the weathered wall.

The squawking and flapping continued.

Ellie looked in. Three hens in the upper right corner of the coop were especially agitated.

Ellie sniffed. Her tail was down. The hair on the back of her neck stood like bristles in a brush.

She backed her paws down the side of the coop and stood three or four feet to the right. She knew that being patient was the key to solving this matter.

Then suddenly, when she felt that the time was right, she barked!

Lucy sprang from the window!

Ellie could have taken her down easily, but she knew better. Instead, she let the cat pass, and watched as Lucy leaped toward the barn.

Lucy darted behind the garden tiller.

Ellie stared, waiting to see what Lucy would do, but she knew that the irritating cat had already been reckoned with.

Lucy crouched low and twitched her tail. Her eyes were filled with fear. Still, she was grateful that she had outrun the big dog.

Ellie approached the small house again. She poked her nose in, sniffed, and listened. Her round eyes surveyed the coop from top to bottom and from corner to corner. Hens of different colors were nesting peacefully again.

She dropped away from the window and began walking toward the vegetable garden that was just on the other side of the tractor shed. The dog had her mind set on making sure that everything was right on every square inch of that farm!

The Special of the Day was Meat Loaf, Mashed Potatoes, and Green Beans.

Kate stuck by her chicken salad sandwich idea, and was glad that she had. It too, was delicious.

Mike tipped the waitress and paid the lunch ticket at the counter.

Kate went to the Ladies' Room to wash up.

She combed her bangs and took one more look at her pretty little face in the mirror. She smiled. They would be home in less than an hour. She was glad they were ahead of schedule.

Ellie slept as the rooster pecked at the few remaining pieces of dry food in her dish.

Lass was dreaming of bright new bows for her beautiful ears while Holly snoozed near Cap.

Angus walked to the front of the porch. He hoped Kate would bring him a good snack from town — like raisin bread — or cheese. He thought about chunks of tuna — right from the can — and made up his mind. He would beg her for something good tonight.

Suddenly, something caught his eye from the middle of the yard.

Angus put his paws on the porch rail. He leaned forward to get a better look. "What is *thaa-at?*" he whispered to himself.

The thing stared at him.

Angus stared back.

The animal was much larger than he. It had a dark face with bright eyes. Its tail was bushy — with ringed markings. Its paws were hand-like.

The raccoon sat, motionless.

Angus glanced at the gate. Without hesitation, he scratched and dug his way up. His body toppled over it and landed on the second step.

He scrambled to his feet and yapped, sounding out a warning to the animal — but to his surprise — the raccoon was *gone*!

Cap raced to the gate and stood on his hind legs. He saw Angus, who was now on the front walk! *"Angus?"* he said.

Angus seemed not to hear.

"Angus! How did yoo get out *ther-rre*? Get *back* her-r-re! Yoo get back her-rr-re *right now*, Laddie!"

Knowing she'd be safe there, the raccoon had climbed a tree. She looked down at the frantic little dogs.

Cap's fur bristled. "Angus, yoo'd better-r doo as I *say*, or yoo'll be in big tr-rouble!"

Holly called out. "Come back here, Angus!"

Lass whimpered as Angus nosed his way toward the edge of the dirt lane.

Cap eyed the disobedient pup, but Angus just kept sniffing, searching for the thing. *"Angus*! Yoo get back her-rr-e this *instant*!" he snapped.

Angus turned and looked at the porch, where Cap and Holly and Lass stared at him from behind the rail.

He grinned.

He was *free* —

— free to *explore*!

Part Two

~ The Search Begins ~

Cap knew he had to go after him — but he had a bad feeling about going over the gate. He remembered the scoldings he had gotten for going too far from the porch. He had frightened Katie. He had been a *bad dog*! He had made her worry. He did not want to do that again.

Ellie's tags jingled as she walked along the garden's edge.
She was not usually allowed in it, but she knew that if she stepped carefully it would be alright.

"Wonder why *that's* on," Mike mumbled.
"What?" Kate asked.
"The "Check Engine" light is on."
"Maybe it's the battery," Kate said.
"No. It can't be that."
"Maybe we need *oil*?"

"No. That's not it, either," Mike said, still watching the light.

They drove farther down 16.

Mike listened to the engine. It seemed to be running okay, but he would be sure to have Don's Auto take a look at it.

Lass whined.

"Lass," Holly whispered. "It will be alright. Don't worry, Dear."

Cap yipped for Ellie. He listened. He yipped again.

Lass sniffed and perked her ears. Her whiskers were mussed but she didn't care.

Cap had hoped to hear Ellie come running, but he heard nothing but the twittering of the birds in the maple tree.

Lucy twisted and turned through the tall stretch of Iris leaves that grew along the end of the porch. She kept herself hidden so none of them would see her.

Angus scampered along the soft dirt road that led to the highway in the distance. He did not know that this was Briar Lane, the lane that led away from the farm and on to Ken Johnson's place. All he knew was that he was free!

Ellie found it in the tall grass that grew close to the small building. She wondered if it would be alright to chew it—for just a little while. She placed her huge mouth around the heel and bit into it.

The shoe tasted of rawhide—like the treats that Mike often gave her.

Lass sat on the milk crate, watching Cap and Holly as they paced from one end of the porch to the other.

"I just don't know what got intooo that young'in," Cap said sadly, as he shook his head. "He shoulda known better-r-r than ta doo a cr-razy thing like *that!*"

"Oh, Cap. He'll be back before we know it!" Holly replied, trying to comfort him. "He's *young*, but he knows how to take care of himself. He'll be back soon."

"It's *my* fault. What will Katie say?"

"It's not your fault, Cap. It's *no one's* fault. It's one of those things that just *happens*," Holly explained.

"What should we doo, Holly?"

"*We'll* find a solution. Don't worry," Holly said, wondering if she sounded convincing.

"It's *my job* tooo take car-r-re of him," Cap said, his voice filled with guilt.

Holly's head ached. *She* was the oldest, and it was *she* who felt responsible. Angus was too young to be out on his own. Did he know about *cars*? What if he were to get *lost*? What if he were to be out after *dark—all by himself?*

The sun sat at four o'clock in the sky. Angus had finally tired of his game of Hide and Seek with the grasshopper that had suddenly appeared in the tattered grass.

He walked along the path that twisted and wound its way through a small woods. He sniffed as he walked along, hoping to find new adventure with each and every turn!

Lucy could barely contain herself. She wanted to dart off and look for that little *yapper*. She surely did!

She twitched her tail. She could see him in her mind's eye — that scrawny, *poor-excuse-for-a-dog,* pup! She could hear herself *hissing* at him. She could see the *fear* in his eyes —

Then she thought of *Ellie* —

She knew the consequences of her actions could be quite serious.

Cap made his announcement. "I'm going out ther-r-rre!"

"I'll go with you," Lass said, her voice shaking.

"No!" Holly shouted. "You don't know this farm as well as I. *I'm* going! You two stay here, and wait for Mimi and Mike!"

Cap sighed. He knew that he had to tell her — his oldest, best friend. "I don't want tooo hur-rr-rt your-r-r feelin's, Holly, but yoo have no *business* being out ther-rre! Angus may have r-r-run tooo far-r-r! Yoo shouldn't bur-r-den your-rrself so, Ma'am!"

"I *know* this farmland, Cap. I'm *going,*" Holly said again.

Cap cleared his throat. "Holly! Yoo might know this *far-r-rm*, but yoo don't know what's *past it*, Ma'am!"

"And you *do*?" she asked.

The brindled dog looked at her squarely, but he spoke softly. "*I'm* going, Ma'am."

Lass looked at Cap. "I'll help you, Cap! I can *do* it!"

Cap frowned. "No, Lass! We can't ar-rgue aboot this! Time's *a' wastin'!*" He barked, and listened for Ellie.

Lucy twitched her ears. Her eyes gleamed as her mind raced.

"Lass! If yoo can make it off the por-rrch, find *Ellie*! Tell her-rr what has *happened*! Tell her-rr tooo check the pond, the shed, and the outer-r-rr edge of our-rr place!"

Lass nodded.

"Then come back her-r-re and wait with Holly. I'll trr-ry tooo find him and be back as *fast as I can!*"

"Okay. '*Got* it!" Lass said.

"Holly, yoo stay her-r-re, and wait for-rr Katie and Mike! If they come back anytime soon, yip and *yip*! Trr-ry tooo lead them towar-r-rrd the dirr-rt r-road! Let them know it's an *emer-r-rrgency!*"

"The dirt *road*? The one that leads to the Johnson place?" Holly asked.

Cap nodded.

"*Why?*"

"Because that's wher-rrre I'm going tooo star-rr-rt lookin' for-rr him. If he's gone that way, he could be in *r-rr-real danger-r-rr!*"

As Mike drove, his mind was on the chores that were waiting for him at home. There was always work to do—

animals to care for, eggs to gather, fences to repair, gardens to weed, tillers to fix, barns to clean, and fish to catch.

The pick-up lunged forward.

Kate looked at her husband. "What *is* it, Mike? 'Any idea?"

"I don't know. We have plenty of gas. I checked the oil the other day, so I'm sure it's okay too," he said as he looked at the dash.

"What are we going to *do*?"

"Well, the best thing to do is to get 'er home, and call Don in the morning and have him take a look. Something's wrong here."

"Do you think we can make it home?"

"We're going to have to," he said.

Angus leaned forward and sniffed the smelly thing. He bumped it with his nose and waited to see what it might do.

To his surprise, the smelly thing did nothing.

Angus bumped it again and waited.

The smelly thing didn't move.

Angus yapped at it and turned it with his paw.

It sat, motionless.

The pup whined.

For the life of him, Angus couldn't get that turtle to come out of its shell!

Cap had hoisted himself over the gate on his second try, but Lass had never done this before.

She studied the gate.

Holly watched as Lass approached it and backed away.

Holly started to speak, but Lass tried again and fell back onto the floor.

"Lass, Dear. It's alright. *You* don't have to. *I* can get over that gate. I *know* I can. *You* stay here and wait for Mimi and Mike. I'll find Ell—"

"*No!*" Lass shouted, as she ran as fast as she could, making another run at it. This time she pushed and grunted her way up!

She fell forward onto the porch steps with a thud.

Holly craned her neck over the top of the gate. "'You *okay*, Dear?"

Lass got to her feet. "I *think* I am!" she said.

Holly could see that she wasn't hurt. She wasted no time. "Lass! *Go find Ellie!*"

Lass stared. Holly had never yelled at her before.

"*Go!*" Holly commanded.

"Okay! I'll find her, and tell her what's *happened!*" Lass barked.

"*Hurry!*" Holly shouted.

Lass ran toward the back of the house, screaming. "*Ellie! Where are you? Ellie! We need you!*"

Her curiosity had gotten the best of her. Without being seen, Lucy made it to the edge of the dirt road.

She hoped to track them—those irritating dogs!

Kate and Mike were on the side of the two-lane highway with the hood up on the truck. Mike had turned the flashers on and was looking at the engine.

Kate waited, anxiously.

Mike checked this thing, that thing, and everything he could think of, but he found nothing unusual.

The "Check Engine" light was still on.

Cap had slowed his pace from a run to a walk. He looked in all directions as he made his way down the edge of the dirt road calling for the lost pup.

Angus heard nothing. He was nowhere near, and was having the *time of his life*!

The old shoe lay next to her in the grass and Ellie was snoring.

She was dreaming — dreaming of chasing Lucy.

Lucy listened as Cap called, "Her-r-rre Angus! C'mon, boy! Let's go *home*!"

Somehow, the cat was frightened of the thought of confronting him now, and the blood rushed through her as she darted away.

Lass had checked the back yard, the chicken coop, and had now made her way to the barn.

She found a loose board and poked her head in. The barn smelled of hay and of Judy and Rex. There was also the faint smell of Lucy.

She nudged her way through the opening and ran to Judy's stall. The horse moved her ears forward and looked in Lass' direction.

Lass was so frightened that she thought she might be ill. Judy was so—*large!*

Judy stared at Lass with gigantic eyes. "What are you doing way out *here?*" she asked the short-legged dog.

"I'm looking for Ellie. Have you seen her?"

"Well, not since noon. She stopped by *then*, but she hasn't been back since."

Lass frowned.

Judy called over to Rex. "'You seen *Ellie* around lately?"

"No, I *haven't*," Rex replied, switching a fly with his tail. "Not since this morning. Sometimes she sleeps by the hay bales though. You might want to check there."

Before Judy had the chance to say a word, Lass spun around and ran toward the hole in the side of the barn. "Thank you very much for your help!" she called over her shoulder.

She made her way through the opening and was gone.

"'Never see those little dogs out here. 'Wonder what's goin' on?" Rex said.

"'It's *very* odd. 'Don't *know*," Judy replied.

A blue station wagon pulled in front of the red truck. A young man got out of the car and talked to Mike for a few minutes. He got back into the car and left.

"What's he doing?" Kate asked as he drove away.

"He's going to see if his dad can help us," Mike happily replied as he climbed back into the driver's seat. "He says they live just down the road."

Angus sat near the oak tree and watched her — the yellow dog in the distance. He did not know what it was that she had, but his mouth watered as the dog rolled and chewed the bone.

Suddenly, a voice called. "Sadie! Come, girl!"

The dog grasped the bone in her teeth and ran to the back of the house.

Angus' stomach felt hollow. He could not help but wonder if the yellow dog had left something good behind — a bite of something — a crumb of something —

He looked at the strange house and whined, but hungry as he was, he ignored his hunger. His instinct told him to leave that place.

The pup looked north, south, east, and west. He made his best guess and started walking in the direction of where he thought home might be.

Ellie was nowhere to be found, and Lass ran through it again in her mind. She had checked the picnic table, the chicken coop, the tractor shed, and the barn. She had talked to the horses and had looked near the hay bales.

She walked around the foundation of the house and started up the front steps.

"Lass! Did you tell her what's happened?" Holly asked, wagging her tail.

"Holly?" Lass said. "I can't find Ellie *anywhere!* I can't imagine where she's *gone!* I've looked and *looked* for her! I don't know what to *do!*"

"She'll be along, Lass. Don't worry," Holly said softly.

"But you and Cap were counting on me!"

"Sshh, Dear. Come here," Holly whispered.

Lass stepped onto the top step.

Holly leaned as far forward as she could. "It will be alright. We'll listen for her. Not to worry, Dear. *Not to worry.*"

The blonde boy glanced at his wrist. It was past three. He hated that he was running late. He pedaled faster.

His shirt tail flapped in the breeze as he wheeled along the path that led to the edge of Mr. and Mrs. McKinney's farm.

After rounding the last corner, he slowed down. He didn't want to spook the horses.

Matt Johnson walked his bicycle to the side of the old barn. He leaned it against the splintered wood and walked around the hitching post. He opened the barn door. "Hey, Judy! Hey, Rex!" he said.

Judy pawed the ground.

"I'm runnin' late. I *know*," Matt admitted.

Judy whinnied low as he took her by the halter. He unlatched the stall gate and led her out of the barn.

He took an apple from his pocket as they walked to the pasture. He opened the gate and led Judy in. "Here ya go, Judy!" he said, giving her the sweet apple.

Judy took the apple and swished her tail.

Matt latched the gate and returned to the barn for Rex.

Matthew handed him the red-green apple. Rex chewed methodically as Matt took hold of his halter and unlatched the gate.

Rex followed obediently, hoping for another.

Matt led him through the gate. He grinned and patted the horse's neck. "Judy's out there! *Go on!*"

Rex waited for a moment—but there were no more apples.

"Go *ahead*! She's *waitin'* on ya!"

Rex neighed softly to him.

Matt grinned at the beautiful horse. "Be *good!*" he said, as he latched the gate.

He looked at his watch. He had two more chores to finish at his place before homework.

He hopped on his bike.

"'Algebra quiz tomorrow," he thought to himself as he began pedaling. "'Not my best subject."

Judy whinnied in the distance.

Matt knew they were glad to be out for the afternoon.

To tell the real truth, Cap was getting very worried. He had grown weary of trying to find Angus, and he knew that the situation was growing worse with every minute that passed.

"Young'ins sur-rre ar-r-re a lot of *tr-r-rouble*," he whispered to himself.

Lucy watched Cap from behind the bushes that grew near the rusty wire fence. She wondered if she should approach him.

Cap stopped and listened as Lucy twisted her way through the brush. The hair stood down the center of his back. He growled low.

The cat stopped. She sat, keeping a safe distance between them.

There the brindled dog stood with his eyes fixed upon her.

Lucy stared back, showing no emotion.

Cap took two steps toward her.

Lucy remained calm and spoke. "'Lost Angus, *huh*?" she asked, already knowing the answer.

Cap growled again. *"I don't have time for-r-r the likes of **yoo**!"* he said.

"Don't growl at me," she replied, matter-of-factly, not revealing the fear that he had just stirred within her. "'Want me to help you *find* him?" she asked.

*"I don't need no help fr-rom a **cat**!"* he said, turning away from her.

Lucy still sat. "'Suit yourself," she said.

Cap took a deep breath. "Have yoo *seen* him?"

"Maybe. Maybe *not*," she said, looking through slanted eyes.

"Well, *have yoo*, or-rr-r *not*?" Cap demanded.

Lucy eyed the dog.

"*Lucy! If yoo've har-rr-rmed him, in any* **way**—!" Cap warned.

"No, Cap. I haven't seen him."

Cap lowered his head and sighed.

"But I'll help you find him, if you *want me to*," she said.

Cap studied her.

Lucy smiled. She smiled a genuine, friendly smile.

"Yoo *mean* that, *don't* yoo?" he said.

"Mean *what*?"

"That yoo will *help* me."

"Yes. I *do* mean it, Cap. I *will* help you."

"Well, tooo tell yoo the trr-r-ruth, Lucy, I could use some help aboot now. *I've looked and looked*, and have had *no luck*! 'No luck, *what-so-ever-r-rr*!"

"He could get lost out here. We need to *find* him."

"Yes. We doo," Cap agreed.

"What do you think we should *do*, then?" she asked.

"I'm not rr-really *sur-r-re*," Cap admitted.

Lucy thought for a moment. "How about *this*? I'll go toward the brushy lane and look. You take the opposite direction. We can comb a lot of area in a fairly short time that way."

Cap nodded. "Okay. *Yes*. That sounds like as good'a plan as *any*."

"If I find him, I just take him *home*?" she asked.

"*Aye*. And, *I'll dooo the same*."

"And, if we *don't* find him?" Lucy asked.

"We have tooo find him, Lucy. We *have* tooo."

"Well, let's get started," she said, getting to her feet.

"*Lucy*?" Cap asked.

"*Yes*?"

"Which way doo I go tooo get back *home*?"

"*That way*, Cap," Lucy nodded. *That way* is home."

"Thank yoo."

Lucy purred. "Good luck, Cap. I hope we find him soon."

"*Aye*! I hope so tooo," he whispered, more to himself than to her.

Ellie opened her eyes and sat up with a jolt! As she looked around she didn't see anything that should have caused her alarm, but she felt uneasy.

She ran to the front of the house and up the porch steps.

"*Ellie*! I've been *looking* for you! *Angus*! He's *gone*!" Lass shrieked.

"*Yes!*" Holly chimed in.

"Whut do yuh mean, **gone**?" Ellie asked as she looked around. "Wheer's *Cap*?"

"Cap has gone to *look* for him." Holly said.

"He's been gone for a long while! I went looking for you, and I couldn't *find* you!" Lass complained.

"I was down by the work shed," Ellie explained. "Do yuh have any idea a'wheer they are?"

"No," Holly said. "We don't."

"I hope they're not *lost*!" Lass whimpered.

"**I'll** find um!" Ellie shouted.

"What do we do *now*, Holly?" Lass asked, as they watched Ellie race down the lane.

"Wait," Holly replied. "We'll just have to *wait*, Dear."

Part Three ❀ ❀

~ The Hole ~

"Hi! I'm Bill Dawson. You've already met my boy, Joe," the older man said.

"Hello! We're Mike and Kate McKinney," Mike said, shaking hands with the man. "It's nice to meet you."

"'Nice to meet you too," Bill replied. "Well, let's give it a listen," he said.

Mike started the engine.

"It sounds like it'll get you to my place," Bill said, after listening for a minute or two. "You can follow us. We're just a little ways down the road."

"We don't mean to put you out," Mike said.

"Aww! It's no trouble a'tall! C'mon. It's not far."

"Well—okay. Thanks!" Mike said, relieved.

Kate smiled at the man.

It was in no time that the McKinney's and the Dawson's were making the right turn that led to Bill Dawson's farm. The lane was lined with wildflowers. Brilliant purples, pinks, and yellows grew on either side.

Sarah Dawson was standing in the front yard as Bill and Mike pulled in.

"'Glad we could be of help," she said, smiling, gesturing for them to come in. "Would you like some coffee? Lemonade? You folks must be tired. Please. Sit down here at the table. Let me get you something."

"Oh, don't go to any trouble, Ma'am," Mike said.

"Oh, goodness! It's no trouble," she said.

Mike grinned. "Well, I would like coffee then, if you have some made already?"

"Yes. Thank you! Coffee would be fine for me too," Kate added.

Mrs. Dawson took four cups from the cupboard and filled them.

Cream and sugar was already on the table.

Bill joined them while Sarah tended to the supper that was cooking on the stove. The men talked of the events of the morning and discussed what might be wrong with the truck.

Mike used the phone and called Don's Garage. He made arrangements for the truck to be towed the next morning. He was thankful that Don was the kind of guy who didn't mind working on a Sunday, every now and then.

The young man was hammering outside.

"Joe's got a project going," Mrs. Dawson told Kate. "'Stay for supper? We have plenty! I'd love it if you would."

"Well, of course, they're going to stay for supper!" Mr. Dawson barked. "These folks are *tired*! They're *hungry*!"

Sarah chewed her bottom lip. She looked at Kate and Mike.

"Well, I suppose everything will be alright at home," Mike said to Kate. "We'll have some hungry animals to feed when we get back, but they'll be no worse for the wear. Kate? Would you like to stay and have supper with these nice people?"

Kate wasn't hungry, but she appreciated their genuine invitation. "Well? Yes! We'd like that very much!" she said.

"*Wonderful!*" Sarah Dawson said, clasping her hands together. "We're so glad to have you!"

The two men excused themselves and walked outside to see how Joe's project was coming along.

Kate watched as Sarah turned the chicken pieces that were frying up to a golden brown in the skillet.

Potatoes were boiling, green beans were simmering, and the oven was heating. Sarah had a pan of freshly cut biscuits ready to bake. A large covered bowl of banana pudding sat on a shelf in the refrigerator for dessert.

Hungry or not, the cooking food smelled wonderful! Kate could see that it was going to be a delicious supper!

Lass had curled up on the top porch step as Holly sat on the other side of the gate.

Holly wondered if Cap and Angus and Ellie were alright. She wondered when they would be home. She missed Mimi and she wanted her supper.

Lass panted. She just couldn't understand how Holly could remain so calm in a situation such as this!

Ellie knew that she had been gone too long from the farm, already. Still, she knew she had to find Angus and Cap. Katie would be heartbroken if they were not there when she returned!

Angus had wandered up through the north end of Ken Johnson's farm. He thought of his water bowl on the porch as he trudged along.

A bird flew overhead. He watched as it grew faint in the distance.

The sun was going down in the west.

"*Hi!*" a voice said from behind him. "I'm **Jumper**! What's *your* name?

Angus spun around in surprise.

The little rabbit smiled a toothy smile.

"I'm *Jumper*! What's *your* name?"

"Uh, I'm *Angus*," Angus said.

"Whatcha **doin'**?" the rabbit wanted to know.

"*What?*" Angus asked.

"Whacha *doin'*? You out here **playin'**?" the rabbit asked.

"Uh, well, *sort of—*" Angus said, not really knowing what to say.

"I'd *play* with ya, but Mama won't **let** me. It's too *late*. It's gettin' **dark**."

"*Yeah*," Angus said, looking at the sky.

"Maybe we could play **tomorrow**! You could meet my *fam'ly*! They're **nice**!" the rabbit said.

"That would be fun, but I need to be gettin' *home*," Angus said.

"Where do you *live*?" the rabbit asked.

"'On Katie and Mike's farm. Do you know where that is?"

"**Nuh-huh**," the little rabbit said.

"*Jumper-r-rrr!*" a voice called from not far away. "It's time to *come in!*"

"*I gotta go! That's **Mama**!*" the rabbit whispered as he hopped toward the hole. "*G'bye!* It was nice *meetin' ya!*"

With that, the little rabbit disappeared.

Young Joe Dawson joined everyone in the kitchen. He opened a can of cream soda and sat listening to the friendly conversation around the table.

The smell of baking biscuits filled the kitchen.

Lucy turned cold when she heard it—that familiar sound.

She knew that her best bet would be to climb a tree but the nearest tree was too far away. She wouldn't make it.

The cat crouched and peeked through the tall grass as she watched the big dog pass.

Ellie seemed to be looking for *something*, but, for some reason, Lucy sensed that the big dog was not looking for *her*.

Angus was no longer interested in exploring and he wandered aimlessly.

His stomach growled at him.

He did not chase the occasional flying insect or grasshopper, and no longer delighted in the thought of finding a wooly brown caterpillar. His thoughts were of home—of his supper—and of nothing else.

Kate had insisted upon helping Sarah with the dishes.

Bill chuckled. "The women sound like a couple of hens — with all that chatter goin' on in the kitchen!"

Mike grinned. "Yeah. They're havin' a *good* time!" he whispered.

Sarah dried her hands and walked into the living room. "I'll bring you two a nice bowl of banana pudding and some more coffee, if you'd like."

"Why, of course, we'd like that!" Bill sputtered. "Why, I wouldn't turn down your puddin' in a million years!" He winked and turned to Mike. "Sarah makes the best banana puddin' you ever put in your mouth! I swear she does!"

Sarah blushed.

"Yep. We'll have some puddin' and more coffee, and then Mike, I'll give you kids a lift home. You said Don's wrecker will be here at nine in the mornin' to get your truck? I hope it's nothin' too awful serious."

"Well, I really do appreciate the fine supper and all the help you've given us, Bill," Mike said earnestly. He reached for his wallet.

The older man frowned at him. "Aww! Put yer money away. 'No need for *that*. Don't think nothin' of it! Why, you'da done the same for *me*! I know you would have!"

"'You sure?" Mike asked.

"Yeah, I'm sure," Bill said.

Angus had come upon the beast that was feeding on green grass near the edge of the pasture quite by accident. He stared at the animal's fat, pink tongue, and the teeth that could tear him in half! He tried not to hear the crushing, gulping sounds the beast made as he chewed and swallowed each mouthful.

The animal had a gigantic, rectangular body. His legs were very bony and thin, and his tail swooshed left to right, then left again.

The rectangular beast stamped his hoof.

Angus jumped.

The bull rolled one large brown eye around and looked at the pup. "What's the matter, sonny? Did I *scare* ya?"

The little dog's body shook as he stared at the bull.

"Well? *Did I?*" the beast asked in a husky, deep voice.

Angus tried to speak but no words would come.

The bull raised his head and said, "Hey, boy? What ya doin' way out *here*? I never *seen* ya before. Where do ya *live*?"

Angus took a deep breath. "I'm n-n-not quite sure, Sir. I think maybe that way?" he said nodding to the east. "Or, is it *that* way?" he said, looking south.

"No, boy! I mean what *farm* do ya' live on! *Huh?*"

"Well, I live with *Katie and Mike*. Do you know where *that* is, Sir?"

The bull swooshed his tail and chewed a spear of grass as he thought. "'Can't say as I do, sonny."

Angus could not hide his disappointment, and the bull wondered what it was that he could *say*, what it was that he could *do*, to help the little fellow.

For a moment, no one spoke at all.

"I'm sorta *lost*," Angus finally admitted.

The bull moved his head forward. "Now, don't you worry about it, kid. You'll make it home okay. You *will*. Honest!"

Angus' eyes filled with tears. He thrust himself forward onto the grass. "I don't *know*, Sir!" he sobbed. "*I don't know about that!*"

"*Hey!* Little fella! It's gonna be alright!" The bull smiled. "Come on. *Get up.*"

Angus stood and blinked the remaining tears away.

"Ah! *That's* better! Now, little fella, you get along! You go and find your way back, son. You can do it! I *know* you can!"

"Do you think so? *Really?*" Little Angus asked, searching his face.

"Sure I do!" the bull said.

Angus grinned. He licked the last tear from his nose. "Yeah, I'll find my way home! I *will*!" he shouted.

"Well, young man, *that's* the spirit!"

"'Nice to meet you, Sir! And — thanks for being so nice to me!"

"You'll do just fine, son! You'll do *just fine*! Take good care of yourself and get on *home* now — an', nice meetin' you too, little fella!"

The bull watched as the little pup made his way along the edge of the fence. He wondered where his home really was.

Angus turned and waved. "G'bye!"

The bull sighed and swooshed his tail. He felt empty inside.

Angus started walking once more.

The bull thought of searching for more good grass to eat, but he just wasn't hungry anymore.

Holly had dreamed about Little Angus. He had come walking down the lane in her lovely dream. They were all there to greet him — Lass, Cap, Ellie, Mimi, Mike, and herself. Everyone wore a bright smile — especially Angus.

Mimi gave everyone beefsteak — and biscuits — with strawberry jelly!

She looked around the porch. She did not see Angus or Cap. Yes, it had been only a dream.

"What time is it, Holly?" Lass asked from the other side of the gate.

"I don't know, Dear," the older dog said.

"I just wish there was something we could *do*," Lass said as she walked to the end of the top step.

"Lass? Come here, Dear."

Lass walked back to the gate.

Holly smiled with kind eyes. "Don't worry so. We just need to wait patiently."

"Holly, do you think they'll *find* him?"

"Yes. I do, Dear. I think they'll be back *any minute*."

Lass turned and faced the dirt road. She stared into the night.

She *wanted* to believe Holly—Oh! How she wanted to!

Angus looked at the periwinkle sky that loomed overhead. Shadows that would all too soon turn to darkness surrounded him.

Lucy had seated herself in a redbud tree. She was three limbs high, just to the left of center.

She looked in all directions, hoping to see any sign of any one of them.

She listened, but she heard only the faint rustle of the leaves in the tree.

Cap's skin turned to goose flesh at the thought of never seeing Little Angus again. His mind reeled with thoughts — bad thoughts of what could happen to him out there.

He pressed on.

Ellie coughed and stopped to rest.

Honestly, Cap could hardly believe his ears! His heart beat with a happy, joyful rhythm. He had heard that wonderful sound many times before! *"Ellie!"* he shouted.

Ellie woofed. "Cap! 'Over **heer**!"

Cap ran through the gnarled grass as fast as his short legs would carry him!

"Hi, Cap," the big dog said, as Cap appeared before her.

"Oh, Ellie! I'm so glad tooo *see* yoo! *Angus*! He's *lost*! We have tooo *find* him! He's out her-r-re somewhere-r-rre, but I don't know wher-rre!" Cap explained, short of breath.

"Yup, Cap. I know! Holly and Lass told me. Have you seen any sign of him anywheer? *Paw prints*? *Grass that's been laid over*? *Anything like that*?" Ellie inquired.

Cap frowned, turning his head at an odd angle. "No-o-o. Nothing!"

Ellie looked at him with her brown eyes set. "Don't worry, Cap. We'll find him."

"I surr-re hope so," Cap replied, doubtfully. "Ellie, it's pr-r-retty da-rr-rk out her-r-re."

"You've been out heer a long time, haven't yuh, Cap?"

"Aye. I *have*, Ellie," he said.

Ellie could see how weary he was. His eyes had lost their shine. "We'll find him, Cap," she said again, softly.

Cap looked at the big dog. She seemed so sure of it.

He wasn't so sure. He wasn't sure of anything anymore.

Sarah gave Kate her recipe for apple dumplings. "This recipe is so easy," she said. "You try it! They're delicious!"

"Mike will *love* these!" Kate said as she read it.

They had decided to stay together in their search for him. Ellie knew the area well and Cap was grateful for that.

"Aaang-gus! Wher-rre *ar-r-re yoo*, young'in?" Cap called, over and over again.

"**Heer Boy**!" Ellie hollered. "We'er gonna take yuh **home**!"

Angus tried not to think of warm beef and gravy in his bowl, but his stomach was growling so!

The tips of his ears were cold and he had picked up a prickly something in his fur just under his right elbow.

He stopped. He grabbed hold of the thing with his teeth. He pulled —

It was at that very moment that he heard something in the night!

"Drip."

Angus cocked his head and listened carefully.

"*Drip*," he heard again.

The pup tiptoed toward the sound.

"Drip!" he heard clearly now.

Angus took two steps forward and found himself next to it—

—a hole in the ground.

He studied it for a moment. He didn't know why, but for some reason, it had been partially covered with a weathered board.

"Drip, drip!" he heard again and again.

"*Water*!" he thought to himself, as he moved his tongue over his dry mouth.

He pushed against the board with his head but the board didn't budge.

He took a deep breath and pushed again, with more strength this time. He managed to shove the board backward.

He craned his scrawny neck, but he really couldn't see much, so he leaned forward just a bit more.

He smelled the sweet smell of the damp earth. He could almost *taste* the cool, refreshing water!

He peered into the darkness, wondering just how deep the hole might be, and then—it happened! His front feet lost their grip and the soil began crumbling—giving way to the ground below!

Angus scrambled, trying to control the earth's tumbling, but it was to no avail! The harder he tried to gain his footing, the faster the soft earth seemed to plummet beneath him!

His heart pounded in his chest as his head began to spin!

Angus felt himself falling—over the edge—*into* the black hole!

Lucy made it down the tree with ease.

She looked at the darkening sky and thought of her corner of the barn. She longed for her soft bed.

Oddly enough, she even missed Judy and Rex.

Angus landed on his back.

He opened his eyes. He saw nothing but darkness — the blackness of the hole around him.

He felt a bump rising on his head. He rubbed it with his paw as the dripping sound echoed in his ears.

He whined and moved a few steps to the right. He looked at the hole from this new angle, trying to make sense of the place that he now found himself in.

"Cap? Holly?" he said.

He felt mud, like cold paste, in his whiskers. He wanted to lick and it was all he could do to keep from it.

"Hey!" he called out. "Can anybody *hear* me?"

He looked at the night sky. Silver stars seemed to wink at him from above.

He stared back at them.

They were so far, far away.

"The world ain't what it once was," Bill was telling Mike. "That's for sure! Why, I remember when we used to go down to the quarry and play when we was kids. 'Can't have fun like that no more!"

Lucy didn't know why, but she had an uneasy feeling. She listened.

Did she *hear* something, or did she just *want* to hear something?

She wasn't sure, but the sound came from behind her it seemed.

She twitched her right ear. There it was—again!

Her eyes gleamed in the night.

She stretched her body and zig-zagged through the grass.

Her long, thin legs carried her closer and closer to the sound that was becoming more audible with her every stride!

Cap and Ellie could see the small moon-lit trees just ahead. The smell of sweet apples filled their nostrils.

Cap smiled. Katie had given him apple slices many times. Apples were *delicious*! They were as delicious as the candy he'd stolen right from the dish that sat on the table by Mike's chair! "*Apples*!" he shouted to Ellie.

"I smell um!" Ellie barked back.

Cap knew there would be apples on the ground. His mouth watered as they raced toward the orchard.

Suddenly, Ellie caught a glimpse of her from the corner of her eye!

Lucy saw the big dog and climbed a nearby fence post, praying she'd be out of reach!

Ellie stood with eyes of fire, glaring at the trembling cat.

Lucy sat with her claws extended. She stared back at the dog that was clearly on edge.

"Angus! Is that *yoo*?" Cap called ahead.

"*No*! It's that **cat**!" Ellie yapped back. "It's **Lucy**! She's on the **fence**!"

Lucy did not move. She knew she had no way of escaping and she mentally prepared herself for the fight.

"*Ellie*! Don't *har-r-rm* herr-r! She's looking forr-r-r Angus *tooo*! She's *helping* us!" Cap screeched.

Ellie blinked in surprise.

"Lucy! Have yoo *seen* him?" Cap asked, out of breath, as he came alongside them.

"I haven't found him, Cap. I'm *sorry*. I've searched and searched!"

Ellie stepped back. "You're lookin' for him **too**?" she asked, befuddled by the thought of it.

"Yes, Ellie. I *am*. I've looked everywhere! I haven't spotted him, or any trace of him!"

Ellie studied the cat. She was telling the truth.

"I'm *sorry*," Lucy said again, her voice filled with sadness.

"It's okay," Ellie said with a sigh. "We'll rest fer a minute, and then we'll git started a'gin."

Lucy jumped down from the fence post and Cap seated himself next to her. He no longer noticed the aroma of sweet apples.

Lucy's whiskers twitched as she moved her ears forward. There was that *sound* again — that almost haunting *sound* — "Do you hear *that*?" she asked them.

The dogs arched their necks and opened their ears wide.

Cap heard nothing but the gentle rustling of delicate branches that came from the orchard. "Hear-r-rr *what*?" he asked.

"Ssshh!" Ellie said as she concentrated.

The big dog stood.

Cap and Lucy watched her with great interest.

Ellie cocked her head and raised her brow. "Yup!" she said. "It's **him**!"

Part Four

~ Going For A Ride ~

Joe had taken a very large bowl of banana pudding to his room. He spooned the delicious pudding into his mouth as he watched his favorite show.

He thought of his project. He wondered if Tim, his best friend from the next farm over, would be by.

Lass whined.

"What is it, Dear? What's wrong?" Holly asked.

"Oh, *nothing*," Lass said. "It's just that it's been such a long time that Cap and Ellie have been gone!" She looked at Holly, waiting for a reasonable explanation.

Holly had come up with one. "Yes Dear, it *has* been a long time, but we still need to be patient. Sometimes it takes a while for these things to work out—sometimes, *quite a while*—but they *will*," she said.

"I suppose you're right," Lass said, as she plopped down on the top step. "I'm *hungry*, Holly. 'Wonder where *Katie* is?

I wonder why they're so *late*. It's *dark*, and we haven't had our *supper*!"

Holly walked to her blanket. She picked up the chew bone that was lying there and carried it to the rail's edge. "Here, Lass," she said, nudging it through the small space. "Maybe *this* will help."

Cap stopped to catch his breath.

"C'mon, Cap. We got tuh get tuh Angus," Ellie said.

Cap looked at his legs — the very short legs that could not possibly keep up with hers. He looked at the big dog, filled with guilt.

"I'm not mad at yuh, Cap. *I* understand," Ellie said, "It's just that we need tuh keep *movin'*."

"We'll find Angus quickly enough," Lucy said to Cap, trying to comfort him.

"I'm *tr-r-rrying* tooo keep up! I *am*! But, tooo tell yoo the *tr-r-ruth*, I'm just tooo *tir-r-red*."

"It's alright," Lucy whispered.

"But we've got tooo get tooo him!" Cap complained, frustrated with himself.

Ellie thought for a moment. She stretched her body onto the ground. "Cap? Climb on!"

Lucy and Cap glanced at each other, not knowing what to think.

"Come on, Cap! *Climb on*! Lucy? *You too*!"

Lucy was somewhat frightened of the idea.

"We'll all git there a lot faster that a'way!"

Lucy eyed the big dog and tried to put her fear aside.

"Let's git a'goin'!" Ellie insisted.

"Can yoo car-rr-ry *both* of us?" Cap asked.

"Yup! I *kin!*"

Cap shrugged his shoulders. *"C'mon,* Lucy! 'Looks like we'r-r-re goin' for-r-r a *r-rride!*"

Lucy took a deep breath and lined up behind Cap.

Cap climbed onto Ellie's sturdy back. He grasped her collar with his front feet. He wedged them between the leather and her dense, wooly coat. He nodded to Lucy.

The cat hopped up. She grabbed Cap's coarse fur with her paws, but she kept her claws in.

Ellie stood, almost effortlessly.

"Arr-re yoo r-rready?" Cap whispered to Lucy.

"Yes," Lucy whispered back.

"We'rr-re r-rready!" Cap announced.

Ellie nodded. She sprang forward.

Cap rested his head upon Ellie's right ear while Lucy leaned around his left shoulder.

Ellie ran, taking long, smooth strides.

The breeze blew Cap's whiskers and Lucy felt the chill of the night air on her back.

Ellie spread her toes. Her large feet mashed through the long grass and coarse gravel as she ran.

Lucy stretched her neck forward and she peered into the shadowy night.

Ellie concentrated on just two things — keeping Cap and Lucy secure on her back — and getting to Little Angus!

Soon, Angus' voice echoed from somewhere nearby. *"... Anybody?"*

"We'er **comin'**, Angus!" Ellie hollered out.

Holly felt like crying—something she hadn't done for a long time—but she knew that she couldn't. She had to be strong—for Lass.

Angus raised his brow. It was *Cap*! It was *Ellie* too! —And Lucy? Was that *Lucy* with them?

Ellie kept her pace.

Angus put his front paws on the dirt wall. "I'm down here!" he screamed.

"We're comin', little young'in!" Cap yipped, sounding like a cowboy in a Saturday movie.

Ellie could smell the hole now. She made the corner, slowing just enough to keep Cap and Lucy square on her back.

Cap smelled the hole too. His joy immediately turned to fear.

Ellie stopped. "Okay. Let's go *see*," she whispered.

Cap and Lucy eased themselves off the big dog's back.

"I wonder what has *happened*," Lucy said.

Cap was so filled with worry that he could not speak.

They tiptoed toward the hole.

"Angus?" Ellie called.

"*Yeah?*"

Ellie poked her muzzle between the board and the rim of the deep hole. She could barely see him, but she smelled the little pup. "Are yuh *hurt*?"

"I'm *okay*, Ellie."

Ellie eased forward a bit more. "Are yuh *shure*, Angus?"

"Yeah, I'm *sure*."

"That's good tuh **heer**!" Ellie exclaimed, her voice echoing into the night.

Lucy purred with delight!

Cap barged in, bumping the big dog. "Excuse me, Ellie! I want tooo *talk* tooo him!" He stuck his head in. "Angus! Ar-r-e yoo *alr-r-right*, Boy?"

"Cap?"

"Yes, it's Cap. I'm *her-rre*, young'in."

Angus was afraid to ask, but he had to know. "Are you *mad* at me?"

Cap looked into the hole. He cleared his throat. "No, Boy! None of us arr-re mad at yoo," he said.

"*Really?*"

"Aww! Nobody's mad at yuh, Angus!" Ellie said. "We'er jus' happy we found yuh! We'er jus' happy yuh ain't hurt!"

"That's right, Angus," Lucy said.

"Now, we'er gonna get yuh outta this hole!" Ellie said, knowing there was work to be done.

"Then, we'rr-rre going tooo take yoo *home!*" Cap chuckled.

"Good!" Angus said. "I don't *like* this place!"

Ellie looked at Cap and Lucy with a set jaw. "Stand back!" she said.

Cap and Lucy watched as Ellie dug frantically with her front feet.

But—Angus soon heard them—the clods of dirt that were plummeting toward him!

Lucy sensed that something was wrong. "Ellie! Wait!" she cried.

Ellie stopped digging, but her feet slipped in the damp dirt and the black earth kept tumbling!

Angus closed his eyes—too afraid to look!

Ellie found her footing. "Stay put!" she said to Cap and Lucy. "'Don't want nobody tuh get hurt!"

She called down to the pup. "'You okay down there?"

"Yeah, Ellie, I'm *okay*, but the dirt is fallin' in!"

65

Ellie frowned at Cap. "This ain't gonna *work*," she whispered.

Lucy twitched her tail nervously and Cap swallowed hard.

"Hold on just a minute!" Ellie hollered to the pup.

Lucy looked at the hole. "What are you going to *do*?"

"I *don't* know," Ellie said.

Lucy felt a knot tighten in her stomach.

Angus waited—listening.

Ellie motioned for someone to do something.

Lucy walked to the edge of the hole. "*Angus?*" she said softly.

"*Yeah?*"

"Don't worry. We'll get you *out*."

"Okay—but *how*?" he asked.

The three of them stood motionless. It's difficult to say who wore the sadder face.

Lucy looked at the hole again. A shiver went through her body.

"Hey! Can you get me *outta here*?"

Lucy, Cap, and Ellie looked at each other. No one had the heart to tell him.

Lass' jaws ached from chewing on that bone.

Holly had tried to get Lass to play a guessing game to take her mind off things, but she didn't want to.

"Lass?" Holly asked.

"Yes?"

"Would you feel better if I came outside the gate? I could *sit* with you, then."

"No. Please. Just stay there, Holly. I'm alright."

"Are you sure, Dear?"

"Yes."

"Well, if you change your mind —"

"*I'm* okay, Holly."

The night air was brisk. Lucy fluffed her fur and thought about the situation.

"Whut do we do now?" Ellie whispered.

"Are ya still *up there*?" Angus called.

"Yes, Angus. We're here," Lucy said.

Cap motioned for Ellie and Lucy to follow him to a spot where Angus would not hear.

They huddled together. "We can't just *dig our-rr-r way in,* Ellie. We've got tooo think of a way tooo get *doon ther-rr-re,* without letting the dir-rr-rt fall in," Cap whispered.

Ellie leaned to one side. "*Maybe —* " she whispered, "Maybe we could get a long stick er somethin' — and lower it down *intuh the hole.* Then, the three of us could pull him *up!*"

Lucy blinked. "That might *work!*" she said glancing around, hoping to spot one.

Cap thought more about it. "*I* have an idea," he said.

"*What?*" Lucy asked, as Ellie looked at him inquisitively.

"Ellie? Doo yoo know *wher-rre* we ar-r-rre?"

"Yup," Ellie said.

"'Yoo *sur-rre*?" Cap asked.

"I'm shure."

"How long would it take yoo tooo go back tooo our-rr place, doo yoo suppose?"

"Why?" Ellie asked, studying Cap.

"How long?"

"'Bout twenty minutes, if I hurry."

"Okay! Then that's the *answer-rr-r!*"

"*What's* the answer?" Lucy and Ellie asked, at once.

Cap grinned, his eyes twinkling in the night. "The *tir-rre!* The one with the *r-rr-ope* tied tooo it!"

Ellie mulled it over in her mind.

"*Ooooh!* That's *it!*" Lucy cried. "It will work! That's a *wonderful* plan—with a capital W!"

"**Huh**?" Ellie said.

"Your *tire*, Ellie!" Lucy squeaked at the big dog. "We could lower *that* down to Angus!"

"**Okay!**" Ellie said, taking the cat's word for it.

Cap ran to the rim of the hole. Ellie and Lucy followed just behind.

Lucy sat at its edge as Ellie and Cap leaned in. They shouted down to Angus. Ellie's voice was booming. "Hey, Angus! We got it! We got the **answer**!"

"Young'in!" Cap screeched. "We'r-rre going tooo get yoo *out*, Boy! Ellie's going tooo get her-r *tir-rre* for-r-r yoo tooo grab on tooo! We'r-rr-e going tooo pull yoo up—as quick as anything!"

"*Okay!*" Angus called up.

"I'll go 'n git it, Angus, and I'll be right back! Don't worry!" Ellie said.

"I'll be here!" Angus shouted.

Ellie looked at them. "Cap? You stay heer with Angus. Lucy? Yuh wanna go back with *me*?"

Lucy looked into Ellie's big, round eyes. She realized she had nothing to fear of that dog—that big, truly wonderful, dog! "Well, quite honestly, I probably wouldn't be of much help to you here. I could at least tell Holly and Lass that Angus will be home soon. They must be worried."

"Yup. I'm shure they are," Ellie agreed. "You can let um know he's okay."

"I'll tell them," she said, smiling a genuine, friendly smile.

Cap nodded. "*Aye.* Yoo go back, Lucy, and we'll be meetin' yoo di-r-r-rectly!"

"Okay. You two be *careful*," Lucy said.

"We will," Cap said with a wink.

"We'll git it done!" Ellie said. "Let's git a'goin', Ma'am."

Lucy jumped onto Ellie's back.

Ellie looked at Cap. "All yuh need tuh do is *talk* tuh him. Talk tuh him so he won't be *skeered* down there."

"*Aye!* I'll keep him good company!" Cap said. "*Lucy?*"

"*Yes, Cap?*"

"Thank yoo."

"Well, I wasn't much help, I must say. *And,*" she said, looking him straight in the eye, "it is *I* who should thank *you — and* Ellie!"

"For-r-rr *what?*"

"For being such good *friends* to me."

"Think nuthin' of it, Ma'am," Ellie said. "I'll be back as soon as I kin, Cap."

Cap watched as Ellie and Lucy disappeared into the darkness.

Lass snapped at a fly that buzzed near her ear. "I wish *Katie* and *Mike* were here!" she whined.

Cap walked to the rim of the hole. "Angus?"

"Yeah?"

"I'm her-rre with yoo, young'in! Don't yoo be scar-r-red doon therr-re. Ellie will be back sooon — ver-rr-ry sooon!"

Part Five

~ The Tire ~

Ellie picked up speed.

Lucy held on tight with soft paws and leaned to the right as Ellie turned onto the path that ran through the woods.

The dog knew this short-cut well. It was just behind the old dirt road near the Johnson's place.

Lucy paid little attention to the branches that hung low. Ellie was able to dodge them almost instinctively.

It was a while before Ellie spoke, but finally she asked, "'You okay up there, Ma'am?"

"Yes. I'm *quite* comfortable, thank you," Lucy said.

"We'll be home in just a bit."

"'Wonderful!" Lucy purred.

Lass was sleeping on the step. She was snoring.

Holly smiled to herself as she listened. Lass would be so upset if she knew!

Sarah Dawson stood on the porch and watched as Mike and Bill loaded the groceries and ice chest into the little blue station wagon.

Kate checked the truck for anything they may have missed while Mike left his truck keys with Sarah. He thanked her for the fine supper one last time.

"I'll be back shortly," Bill said to his wife.

"Okay, Bill. Kate? Mike? It was nice having you! You drop in *any time*, you hear? And, I hope it's nothing too serious with your truck, Mike. Kate, I'll talk to you tomorrow. Drive careful, Bill."

Kate buckled her seat belt and waved good-bye.

Bill started the engine, turned on the headlights, and backed out of the driveway.

Sarah watched until they pulled out onto the hard road. "'Such a *nice* young couple," she said to herself as she opened the squeaky screen door and went back into the house.

Lass sat up with a start. *"Holly?"*

"I'm right here, Dear."

"Are they *home*?"

"No, Dear. Not yet."

"Holly?"

"Yes?"

"What if they don't *come home* tonight?"

"Why, *Lass*! Why would you ask such a question as that?"

"Well, because —"

"Oh, *nonsense*, Dear!" Holly retorted. "I'm sure they're all on their way back by now. I can feel it, Dear. I can just *feel* it."

"Well, I'm *tired*! And I'm *hungry*! I want *Katie*! We're all *alone* here!"

"Lass. *I'm* right here. *You're* right here. So, you *see*? We have each *other*! We're not *alone*, Dear."

This gave Lass little comfort, but she said, "I *suppose*," for what seemed to be the hundredth time.

"*Holly*?"

"Yes?"

"Are there any more bones up there?"

"Yes, I think so, Dear."

"I'm *hungry*!"

"I know, Dear. I *know*."

Bill and Mike talked in the front while Kate watched occasional headlights pass. She couldn't help but think about how helpful Bill and Sarah had been.

Mike laughed heartily at the story that Bill had just finished telling him.

Kate grinned, and thought about the Thank You Gift she would give them — a small centerpiece for their coffee table — or a batch of her "almost famous" peanut brittle.

Ellie was almost to the house when Lass heard it. She looked at Holly with wide eyes. "Holly? Do you *hear* something?"

Holly listened.

Lass looked up the lane.

Holly peered through the porch rail into the shadows.

"I *see* something!" Lass whispered.

"Ssshh!" Holly whispered back. "Let me *listen!*"

"Oh, my goodness! It's *Ellie!*" Lass reported.

The figure came walking toward them.

"Hello! It's me—*Lucy!*" the cat said. "I need to tell you something—something *important!*"

Lass growled and the hair raised on her neck.

Lucy stopped still on the walk.

Holly saw something. She squinted. She could now tell that it was *Ellie*—running *past* the front yard!

Holly yapped for her, but Ellie seemed not to hear. She ran to the back of the house.

"We've found *Angus!*" Lucy said, excitedly. "He's fallen down into a *hole!* Ellie's going to get her *tire* and *rescue* him!"

Holly blinked. She had never heard that cat talk so fast in her life!

"Poo-oo-or Angus!" Lass moaned.

"Is he *alright*?" Holly asked, wide-eyed.

"He's not hurt," Lucy said. "Cap is with him now."

"Oh, thank *goodness!*" Holly said.

"Are The Lady and The Man home?" Lucy asked, looking around.

"No. Not yet," Holly said.

Lass eyed the cat.

"I'm not here to hurt you, Lass. I'm here only to *inform* you."

"You won't hurt *us!*" Lass warned.

"Lass. It's alright, Dear. *Sit down,*" Holly said.

"Thank you for telling us about Angus, Lucy," Holly said.

"Yes, well, I knew you'd be worried," the cat said as she turned and started toward the barn.

"Lass?" Holly said.

"Yes?"

"Tell Lucy *Thank you.*"

"What?"

"Tell Lucy *Thank you* for letting us know about Angus, I said."

"Holly, I *hate* that cat! I'm not going to thank her for *anything*!" Lass whispered.

"Lass!" Holly snapped. "Do *it*!"

Lass took a deep breath. "Hey, Lucy?" she called out.

Lucy turned. "Yes?"

"Thank you. Thank you for telling us about Angus."

"You're welcome. *Very* welcome," the cat said.

Ellie dashed away with the tire clenched in her teeth and the rope trailing past her feet!

Holly blinked back tears of joy. Little Angus would soon be home!

"That'll be fifteen dollars and thirty-eight cents."

"Okay," Bill said as he took a twenty from his wallet.

"Thirty-nine, forty, fifty, and fifty makes sixteen, seventeen, eighteen, nineteen, and one more makes twenty," the cashier said as she gave him his change. "Stop in again, Sir."

"'Sure will," Bill replied with a nod. "Thank ya, now."

He carried the three coffees to the wagon. He handed two of them to Mike. "One with cream, one black," he said.

"Thanks!" Mike said, handing one of the coffees to Kate.

Bill put his coffee in the cup holder. He took a small notebook from the glove box and rummaged for a pen. He noted his gas purchase and mileage. He clipped the pen to the notebook and placed it on the front seat.

Kate took a sip and thought of her loves.

Judy and Rex stood impatiently near the fence.

Rex pawed the ground and whinnied.

Judy looked at the barn. She longed for her stall filled with sweet hay.

"Angus?"

"Yeah, Cap."

"What doo yoo think Katie will give us for supper-r-r tonight?"

"I don't know, Cap, but I hope we have *gravy*!"

"Well, Boy, what ever-r-r it might be, it will su-r-r-rely be *good*, eh?" Cap said.

"Yeah!" Angus said. "*Cap?*"

"Yes, Son?"

"I'm glad you're not mad at me."

"No, Boy. I'm not mad at yoo. Yoo know that, alr-r-ready."

"Do you think *Holly* will be mad at me?"

"I don't think she will be, Boy."

"*Katie! She'll* be mad at me for *sure!*"

"Angus! Stop! No one's going tooo be mad at yoo! We'r-re all just going tooo be happy that yoo'r-rre safe, and well, and *back with us*. Home, boy, *home!* That's the most impor-rrtant thing!"

"I hope you're right," Angus said.

"Listen, Boy. Don't yoo think that I haven't done things that wer-re wr-r-rong too! I sur-r-rely have! That's the way we lear-r-r-rn sometimes, young'in! We doo something *fooolish*! But, what's morr-re imporr-rtant, is that we learr-rn from our-r mistakes—*that we don't r-r-repeat them*! Yoo see? *That's all, young'in.*"

Ellie had stepped on a burr, and the thing had lodged itself between the second and third toe on her back, left foot. A small bead of blood had welled around it but she ignored the pain.

She kept her pace—running hard, breathing deeply, as she ran. Her warm breath billowed out of her nostrils and her chest heaved in and out, in and out, as she pushed herself along the dark path.

"...and, I think he'll be fine, once he's back home," Lucy told them.

"Yeah, I sure hope the little dog's *okay*," Judy said.

"'Sounds like he's been in a heap a' trouble! 'Glad Ellie can help him, that's for sure!" Rex added.

"Well, let us know how he is, will you?" Judy asked.

"Yes. I'll *do* that," Lucy said. "Good night, Judy. 'Night, Rex."

"Get some rest," Judy said.

"I will," Lucy said, yawning.

"Angus?"

"Yeah, Cap?"

"Ar-rr-re yoo still cold, Boy?"

"Yeah—I *am*."

"Well, it won't be much longer-r-r and Ellie will be her-r-re. Yoo be patient, young'in."

"Okay. I'm trying real *hard*, Cap. I'm doin' *al*right."

"Oh!" Kate gasped.

Mike turned and looked at her. "What?"

Bill slowed the car down.

"Oh, I'm sorry, Bill! It's fine. Really! Please. Keep going," Kate said.

Bill pressed on the gas pedal.

"Mike, it's just that I *forgot something*. That's *all*," she whispered, not wanting Bill to hear. "It'll wait, I suppose."

"Forgot *what*, hon?" Mike whispered.

"Well, honey, I think we're very low on dog food, if you can *imagine* it! I, I meant to put it on the list, but I, I guess I wasn't t*hinking*—"

"Don't we have enough to feed them for tonight?" Mike asked, somewhat aggravated with her.

Kate's blank expression told him that they did not.

He frowned. He could not believe that they had done all that *shopping*—

"Maybe there's some in the work shed," Kate said.

"I really don't think so. Kate, that's *your* department! Hon, we'll just have to get by!" he whispered.

78

"Ma'am. That's nothin' to fret about! We can stop right up here at Hines' Market. I'm in no big rush," Bill said, looking at her in the rear view mirror.

"Oh, no! It'll be fine, Bill! I can just—"

"It ain't no trouble, Ma'am. Gracious! We can just scoot right in there, and you and Mike can pick up whatever you need! It won't take but just a few minutes!"

"Thank you, Bill," Kate said.

Mike looked at his watch. It was twenty-five minutes past eight.

Cap heard Ellie. "Angus! Ellie's made it *back*, Boy!"

Angus wagged his tail.

Ellie dropped the tire near the edge of the hole.

Cap could see that she was out of breath, so he did not speak.

Angus cocked his head and listened from below.

Ellie studied her paw. She licked it and felt the burr once more.

She grasped the thing gently with her front teeth. She closed her eyes and pulled. With one tug, the thing was torn away from the pad of her foot.

"Pthewie!" Ellie spat the burr onto the ground.

"Arr-r-re yoo *alr-r-right*, Ellie?" Cap asked, looking at the bloody burr lying in the dirt.

"Shure," Ellie said.

"*Ellie?*" Angus called.

"Hi, Angus! I'm heer!" the farm dog said, cheerfully.

"We need tuh get him outta there," Ellie whispered.

"Aye. It's been a long day forr-rr him," Cap said as he roughed his fur with one shake.

"Well, let's git it done!' Ellie said. She took a deep breath and picked up the tire. She leaned into the hole.

"Uh, Ellie? Wait a minute," Cap said. "Yoo can't just drr-rr-op the tir-r-re doon. The r-r-rope might get away fr-rrom yooo! Yooo arr-rre going tooo have tooo lower-rr-r it doon, slowly — so as not tooo hit Angus or-r-rr anything."

Ellie just looked at the brindled dog.

"We've got tooo pull him up — *on* that tir-rr-re," Cap explained.

Ellie tried to picture it in her mind. "What do yuh think we shud do first?" she wanted to know.

"Well, we need tooo make surr-rr-re that yoo'r-rr-re standin' in the r-r-right spot," Cap began. "Yoo know — a place wher-r-rre it's not so slipper-r-ry!"

"Okay," Ellie said, listening carefully.

"Then, I'll sit on the *end* of the r-r-rope, so it doesn't get *away*!" Cap said. "And, *yooo* can lower-rr-r the ti-r-re doon to Angus!"

Ellie pictured it in her mind. "Okay," she finally said.

"I'll help yoo pull him up when he's on therr-re *good*," Cap said, grinning.

The big dog smiled. "Yup. I think that jus' might do it!"

"Then, we can be on our-rr-r *way*!" Cap chuckled.

"Yup! Let's git it done, then!" Ellie snorted.

Cap motioned for her to follow him. "Wherr-r-re doo yoo think we should position our-rr-rselves, then?" he asked the big dog.

Ellie looked at the rim. She began walking around it, sniffing, searching for the best place from which to bring Little Angus up.

Cap watched her as she surveyed the rim of the hole.

Ellie stopped two-thirds of the way around. "Heer!" she said.

"Ar-rre yoo surr-rre?" Cap asked.

"Yup! This is the spot!"

Cap nodded.

Ellie fetched her tire.

Cap watched as she nosed through the coiled rope, arranging the loop end. "You'll need tuh sit on it right heer, Cap, an' keep it from gettin' away," she instructed.

"Alr-r-rright!"

"'Yuh ready?"

"Let me talk tooo him firr-r-rst!" Cap whispered.

Ellie picked up her end of the loop, nearest the tire. She gripped it in her powerful jaws and stood firm. The tire dangled just below her chin.

Cap leaned in and called down. "Angus! Listen!"

"Yeah?" Angus replied.

"Yoo listen *good*, yoo hear-r me, young'in?"

"I'm listenin'! I'm listenin' good, Cap. *What*?"

"Yoo stand against the back of that hole, Boy! *Way* back! As *far-r* as yoo can get!"

"Okay."

Ellie's going tooo lower-r the tir-rre doon now. She'll tr-rry tooo doo it slowly. 'Don't want it tooo hit yoo or-r anything. R-r-remember! Stand *back*, Boy!"

"Okay!" Angus yelled up. "I'm *back*!"

Cap planted himself on the loop's other end. "Rr-r-ready, Ellie?" he whispered.

"Ready!" Ellie muttered.

Cap took a deep breath as the big dog leaned over the hole and inched forward, just a might more.

"R-r-remember, Ellie. *Slo-oowly*," Cap said.

Ellie nodded and began lowering the tire.

"That's *it*. Don't let go of it."

Ellie lowered the tire slowly, listening to Cap as she did so.

Cap got to his feet, still following the last bit of his end of the loop, making sure that it didn't get away from them. "Angus! 'Yoo okay?" he hollered out.

"I'm okay!" Angus shouted back.

"Alr-r-rright, now! Stay r-rright ther-rre! Wait until we give yoo instr-r-ructions for the next mooove!"

"Okay, Cap!"

Ellie's front paws were planted at the opening of that hole and she was hanging onto the rope with all her muscle!

"Ellie! Yoo'r-r-rre good — just like *that!*"

Ellie stayed put.

"Okay!" "Can yoo r-r-rreach the tirr-re, Angus?" Cap said to the pup.

"No! Not yet!" Little Angus yelled back.

"Trr-rry, young'in!" Cap commanded.

"I *am* trying!" Angus wailed.

"Don't yoo scr-r-ream at me, Boy!" Cap said.

"Well, I *am* trying, Cap!" he whined.

"Ther-rre is no time for-r-r that nonsense! *Gr-r-rab it,* Boy!"

The tire was dangling just above his head. Angus was standing on his hind legs — stretching — reaching for it — any part of it — with his front feet —

"Angus! R-rr-reach!"

Angus felt dizzy. "I'm trying, Cap! Can you get it any closer? Please!"

Ellie's breathing was irregular but she still held on to the last of the rope.

"Ellie? Doo yoo think yoo could get a bit closer-r-r?" Cap whispered.

The Airedale rolled her eyes in Cap's direction. Cap could see that she didn't think she could.

"Ther-r-re's only one thing tooo doo, then," Cap said. "I'll climb doon ther-rre and *get* him out!"

Ellie shook her head, dead-set against the idea.

Cap frowned at the big dog, but Ellie shook her head again.

Suddenly, Cap understood. "I'm *sor-r-rry*, Ellie. *Of courr-rrse*, that won't wor-rrk! Yoo can't pull us *both* out!"

Ellie nodded, this time in agreement.

Cap hollered down the hole. "Angus! R-r-rreach for that tir-re, Boy! Get *on* it! We've got tooo get yoo *home*, young'in! Ellie can't hold on much longer-rr! I'm tellin' yoo for the *last time*! Get *a'hold* of that **tir-re**!"

Angus looked at the tire again. He couldn't—

—or *could* he?

He had an idea!

"Angus?" Cap said, wondering why the young'in was so quiet.

"Tell Ellie to *hold on*, okay?" Angus said.

"We haven't much time, young'in!" Cap warned the pup.

"I *know*!" Angus called back. "Just *give* me a minute! *Okay, Cap*?"

Before Cap could say another word, Angus began scratching up dirt from the back of the floor. He scratched and dug in with his hind feet, making the damp earth scatter as fast as he could! He aimed toward center.

Cap called down. "Whatcha dooin' therr-re, young'in?"

Angus did not stop to answer, but instead, kept scratching and gouging. He clawed at the floor like a wild animal.

Ellie rolled her eyes in Cap's direction. She knew that she was pushing herself to her limit. She couldn't hold on much longer!

Cap could see Ellie's troubled expression clearly in the black night. He knew that she was running out of steam. "He's *dooin' somethin'* down therr-re, Ellie! *Hang on*!" he whispered.

"Angus?" Cap called.

Angus kept scratching and digging into the floor of that dark place.

"*Angus*!" Cap shouted at the little dog.

"Cap! I'm almost finished! I've almost *got* it!" Angus finally said, panting.

"Yoo've almost got *what*?" Cap asked, utterly confused.

"A hill!"

"*What*? 'Can't under-r-rstand yoo, Boy!"

"A *hill*, I said!"

"What in *tar-r-rr-nation* is goin' *on* doon therr-re?" Cap sputtered.

"I'm digging up a *hill* for me to *stand* on!"

Cap looked at Ellie. The big dog could only blink back at him.

"That young'in had better-r-rr *know* what he's *dooin'*, or-r I'm going tooo yank him by the scrr-ruff of his *wee neck*!" Cap said through clenched teeth.

Ellie could not remember when she had ever seen Cap so jittered.

Angus grunted, and suddenly, Ellie felt it. The tire swayed at the other end of that rope!

Angus had tested his balance and was now positioned on top of the hill that he had made.

Ellie waited, but she wondered if she truly could hold on much longer.

Angus stretched his neck to its full length. His heart pounded in his chest as his nose *touched* the tire! He felt, for the first time in a long time, some hope of going home!

Ellie's jaws ached, but she stood, holding tight.

Angus was now standing on the tips of his hind toes. He looked at the tire anxiously. He sprang forward, trying to grab on.

The rope vibrated again and Ellie braced her feet.

"Just one more try and I'll have it!" Angus thought to himself, as he thrust his body toward the tire once more. This time, he managed to grab the tire with his front paws! His hind feet flailed in mid-air!

Ellie felt the sudden tug on the rope as Angus' added weight pulled her head *down* — but she did not falter!

The pup felt as if the weight of the world had just been lifted from his little shoulders! He was off the ground, hanging on, and trying with all his strength to work his way onto the tire.

Ellie felt the jerks and tugs on the rope as Angus struggled fiercely with the thing! She inched her way backward. Ellie knew not to move too hastily.

"When yoo ar-r-re r-rready tooo br-r-ring him up, I'll be helping yoo! I'll pull as *har-r-rd* as I can!" Cap whispered.

"Thanks, Bill," Kate said, as Mike loaded the dog food into the back of the wagon.

Bill opened the car door for her. "No trouble a'tall, Ma'am! 'My pleasure."

Mike looked at the dark sky as he got into the front seat. He would be glad to get home to his evening chores.

Bill drove along thinking about what nice young people they were — Mike and Kate McKinney. He also wondered what was wrong with Mike's truck. He hoped it wouldn't cost Mike too awfully much to have it fixed. You never could tell about those things. Sometimes repairs were reasonable — sometimes they weren't.

He turned on the radio. Country music played softly — a slow song about a heartbroken man who missed his girl.

Cap looked down into the hole and could see that Angus was hanging onto the tire. "He's on therr-re *prr-retty good*, I think!" he whispered to Ellie.

She wagged her tail.

"We'r-rre going tooo star-r-rt pullin' yoo out, Boy! *Don't slip* now!" Cap told the pup.

"Okay! I'll be careful!" Angus said.

Ellie inhaled and began moving backward.

Cap grabbed onto the rope too, with his own vice-like jaws. He moved in a steady slow motion—right along with Ellie.

Ellie was glad to have his added strength. Every little bit helped.

The tire swayed gently, but Angus did not move. He let the tire go where it would.

Ellie pulled and tugged, backing up, little by little.

Cap held on too. He felt the strain on his back and shoulders.

Ellie stopped. She took in a long breath of air through her nostrils.

Cap watched her carefully from the corner of his eye.

Ellie nodded to Cap and started pulling on the rope once more.

Soon, Angus was half-way up the wall!

Cap breathed hard. His ribs billowed in and out as he and Ellie continued moving steadily backward.

Suddenly, Ellie felt a snag!

Angus called up to them. "The tire! It's *stuck*!"

Cap's brows moved forward as he held on with all his might!

Angus hung there motionless, wondering what he should do! He looked from left to right. "I'm holdin' on, but I'm *stuck*!" he warned.

Ellie felt the pup's fear. She braced her feet to keep her good hold and leaned way back this time. The Airedale pulled until her neck muscles bulged!

Cap pulled too, with all the force he could muster!

Ellie raised her brow. She heard the scraping of the tire against the wall of the hole!

"It's *moving*!" Angus yelled to them.

Cap did not say a word. He just kept pulling backward, working in harmony with the big dog.

Ellie clenched her teeth even tighter around the rope and rolled her big eyes toward Cap.

Cap saw the signal and watched Ellie intently.

With one long, last pull — it happened!

Cap could not believe his eyes!

Angus had been flopped over, past the rim of that hole, like a fish that had been caught and pulled onto the bank!

Ellie dropped the rope. The life saver lay on the ground next to her.

Cap looked at Ellie.

"Well, he's outta there, Cap! We got it **done**!" Ellie said.

"*Aye*! We *did*!" Cap said, looking at Angus, glad the job was finished.

Angus made no sound.

Cap leaned forward to get a closer look.

"Don't worry, Cap. He jus' needs tuh get a'hold of his'self fer a minute," Ellie said.

Angus opened his eyes.

"Yoo *okay*, Boy?" Cap whispered, peering at the pup.

"Yeah. I'm *alright*," Angus said.

"Young'in, I sur-rre am glad yoo'rre not *hur-rrt*!" Cap said, relieved.

Angus stood. He looked down at his feet. "I sure am *dirty*!" he said.

Cap and Ellie laughed. Ellie licked the pup's face with her huge tongue.

"Aye! That, yoo ar-rr-re!" Cap agreed. He squared his shoulders. "Well, c'mon, young'in! Let's get yoo *home*!"

Angus looked back at the monster-of-a-hole.

"It's alr-rr-right now, Laddie," Cap whispered softly to him.

"It's late. We better git a'goin'," Ellie said.

"*Aye*," Cap said, with a yawn.

"*Cap? Ellie?*" Angus said.

"Yes, Boy?"

"Uh-huh?"

"Thank you for finding me."

"That's whut best pals are fer, Angus — tuh help out," Ellie said.

"Am I a *best pal*?" Angus asked.

"You bet yuh are!" she said.

"Of cour-r-rrse yoo *ar-rre*, Laddie!" Cap chimed in. "Fr-r-rom the day yoo came tooo us, Boy!"

Angus grinned a wide grin.

"Well, let's git a'goin.' Mike and Katie are back by now, and will be a'worryin' about whut's happened tuh us!" Ellie said.

"I'm prob'ly in big trouble," Angus admitted.

"Naw," Ellie said. "Yure not in no trouble, Angus."

Angus felt ashamed of what he had done. "An', I prob'ly got *you* in trouble *too*," he whimpered.

"Don't *fret*, Angus. They'll *understand* — more than yuh *think* they will," Ellie said, trying to reassure him.

Angus sniffled.

"Hey! Don't yuh *see?*" Ellie said. "They might be disappointed in us once in a while, but *shucks!* They *love* us — *all* of us."

"She's r-right, young'in," Cap said, nodding.

Ellie looked at her tire. "I'll git this in th' mornin'."

"Which way doo we go tooo get back *home?*" Cap asked.

"*That* way," Ellie said, nodding to the south.

It was late. Kate knew she could use the help. "Mike? The clothes need to come off the line. Would you mind helping me with them when we get home?" she asked.

"Okay," Mike said with a sigh. "It won't take but a minute or two, I suppose."

Bill grinned and just kept driving.

Cap was out of breath again.

"Hey, Cap? Why don't yuh hop up heer fer a while? Git a rest!" Ellie suggested.

"Go ahead, Cap! Get a *ride!*" Angus shouted.

Cap frowned, wondering how it was that the young'in could keep up with Ellie, while he couldn't.

"*Aw!* Go on, Cap!" Angus said cheerfully.

Ellie stooped down for him. "C'mon *up.* Take a load off yer feet!"

Cap was so tired that he could not resist. He climbed onto Ellie's back and settled himself in. "We'r-rr-e r-rrunning a wee bit late," he said. "We'd better-rr get mooving!"

Ellie snorted. "Yup! Let's git on home!" she said.

Lucy had curled herself into a furry ball on the step just below Lass. They were sleeping soundly.

Holly looked through the porch rail and listened to the night — the night that was all too quiet.

The turn off to their lane was just ahead.

Kate hummed softly with the radio.

Cap rested on Ellie's wooly back, while Angus, dirty as the dickens, followed right behind. Angus was grateful that he could follow Ellie with her immense paws clearing his way.

Ellie moved steadily toward home.

They had walked some distance, and finally Cap felt better. He tapped Ellie, signaling her to stop.

"Hey, Boy?" he called over his shoulder. "'Yoo tir-rr-red back therr-re?"

Angus came alongside them. "I'm *okay*, Cap," the pup said.

Cap loosened his grip from beneath Ellie's collar and jumped off the big dog's back.

Ellie stretched low to the ground and nodded to the pup.

Angus wondered if he should —

"C'mon up, Angus. You could use a ride too," Ellie said.

With that, Angus wasted no time! He hopped onto the dog's frame and tucked his paws under her collar as he had seen Cap do.

Ellie stood.

Angus' eyes sparkled in the moonlight. "This is gonna be *fun!*" he chirped.

"I'll be r-right behind yoo, Ellie," Cap said. "Let's get home tooo our-r-rr supper-r-r!"

Part Six 🐾 🐾 🐾

~ Their Plan ~

Holly walked to the gate. "Lass! Lucy!" she whispered.

Lass sat up with a jerk. "*What*? Is *Angus* here?" she asked sleepily as Lucy jumped onto the porch rail.

"No! But I think Mimi and Mike are coming down the *lane!*"

"Oh! No! What are we going to *do*?" Lass asked.

"Lass! You and I need to *hide!*" Lucy advised. "'Before they get here! They can't see us here on the steps! You're outside the *gate!*"

"*Yes!*" Holly agreed. "I'll stay quiet on the porch. Maybe they'll think we're *sleeping!*"

"But what if Angus and Cap and Ellie come back *too late*?" Lass whimpered.

"*Ssshh*! We've no time to worry about *that*!" Holly whispered. "Now, go with Lucy and be quiet! *Quiet*, I say!"

Lucy jumped off the rail and motioned for Lass. Lass followed the cat into the blackness under the porch.

Headlights were beaming their way toward the farmhouse.

Holly hid by the wicker chair. She barely breathed as the car passed the front of the house and swung around to the back.

"Don't make a *sound!*" Lucy whispered to Lass.

The strange sounding engine was one that Holly had never heard before! Oh! How she wished that Ellie were here to see what was going on at this late hour!

She heard three doors bang shut. "Three? Why *three*?" she wondered, now trembling with fear.

"Well, Bill..." she heard. It was *Mike* speaking!

"Thank you so..." Her *Mimi* was home!

A wave of relief swept over her. Holly wagged her tail furiously and wanted to bark for her—

—but she knew that she dare not!

"What doo yoo mean that yoo can't step into the edge of the pond? Go *on*, Boy! Yoo've *got* tooo!" Cap said.

Angus turned his back, not wanting to look at the cold, green water.

"Yuh really *shud*, Angus," Ellie said. "Yuh need to wash all that *dirt* off."

"But, I'll really be in big *trouble* if I get all wet in this *water!*" Angus said defiantly.

"C'mon, Angus. *Please*? We need tuh git home," Ellie coaxed.

"*No*! I won't *do it*! I'm not *supposed to*! I'll get all *wet!*" the pup said, sassing the big dog.

Cap squared his shoulders and stood nose to nose with the pup. "Yoo'r-rr-re not supposed tooo get in the water-r-rr, *eh*?" he said, pushing Angus backward. "Well, yoo've got tooo get clean! Make no mistake aboot it, Lad!"

Angus tried to speak, but Cap would not hear of it.

Ellie watched, her eyes focused on Angus' hind feet.

"Now! I'm tellin' yoo! Yoo've got tooo get yoorr-rself a *bath*! Yoo can't go home a'lookin' and a'smellin' like *that*!" Cap sputtered.

"*No!*" Angus screamed.

It was at that instant that Cap muscled-up one lightning-fast, strong-as-an-ox push, and before he knew it, Little Angus was in the water!

Cap looked on as Angus paddled about, working his front feet for all they were worth!

Ellie grinned.

"Ca-aap! Get me *outta here*! It's cold! The water is *cold*!"

Ellie thought the pond looked inviting, but it was late, and she still had chores to do.

"*Ca-aa-ap!*"

"Yoo'r-re not comin' out yet, Laddie! No sir-rrr! Not 'til yoo arr-re clean! *Clean, Mon!*" Cap yelled, over the splashing.

"*Okay!*" Angus shouted back. "I'll get **clean**! But the water is too *cold*!"

Lucy and Lass stayed as quiet as could be. They listened as Kate and Mike and The Stranger unloaded packages from the car that was parked in back of the house, but Lucy also heard something else. She nudged Lass. "*I hear them!*" she hissed.

"What?" Lass asked.

"I hear *Cap*! And *Ellie*! And *Angus*!" Lucy said. "They're *coming*!"

"Are you *sure*?" Lass asked, turning an ear. "*I* don't hear anything."

"Yes! I'm *sure*!" Lucy whispered. "Stay *quiet*, now!"

Lass leaned forward. She hoped to see them, but she didn't.

"*Lass!*" Lucy whispered. "I'm going out to *meet* them! I need to *warn* them! You stay *here!* Tell Holly I'll be right *back!*"

With that, the cat darted off toward the dirt road. She was barely visible in the darkness.

Lass suddenly appeared near the porch steps. "*Holly!* They're coming!" she whispered.

"*Who*, Lass?" Holly asked.

"*Angus*, and *Cap*, and *Ellie!*" Lass said. "Lucy has gone out to *meet* them—to tell them that *Katie* and *Mike* are home!"

Holly looked across the front lawn toward the lane.

Judy whinnied in the distance.

"*I* don't see them," she whispered.

"Well, Lucy *heard them*, Holly."

"...Oh yes, and get the small package behind the ice chest too, will you?" Lass and Holly heard Kate tell Mike.

"Holly! What are we going to *do*? What if Kate comes *out here*?" Lass whined.

"I *don't know*," Holly confessed. "We'll just have to worry about that when the time comes! Get back under the porch, Dear! You mustn't be seen outside the gate!"

"...They have a Stranger with them," Lucy was saying.

"Who is it?" Ellie wanted to know.

"I don't know him," Lucy said. "I didn't recognize his voice."

"*Hmm*," Cap said. "'Wonder what *that's* all aboot, especially at *this* time of night!"

"I'm *hungry!*" Angus whined.

"*Sshh!*" Ellie whispered. "*Quiet*, Angus! We got tuh hurry! We got tuh get tuh that porch—before they *catch us all!*"

Holly turned her right ear toward the front door. She felt helpless as Kate turned on the light!

Before Holly could say a word, Lass jumped from her hiding place! She barked and ran through the front yard. Toward the back of the house she ran, yapping wildly!

Kate heard her! She ran through the house toward the back door. *"Mike! **Mike**! Oh **Goodness**! It's **Lass**! She's **loose**!"* she screamed.

"I *hear* her! I'll *get* her!" Mike yelled from the back yard, where he was already trying to catch the little dog!

But—

—Lass was well ahead of him!

Bill Dawson watched as the small terrier ran past the chicken coop, being followed by Mike, and now, Kate. He grinned, amazed at how fast a little ol' dog like that one could run!

Lucy and Cap and Little Angus crept along the edge of the lane with Ellie leading the way.

Lass' barking grew faint in the distance, but Holly knew that it was only a matter of time before Mike and Mimi would catch her.

Ellie reached the porch first, with Little Angus and Lucy and Cap right behind.

"Lass is *loose*!" Holly told them. "Mimi and Mike are *after* her! They'll catch her any *minute*!"

"Yup," Ellie said. "They'll be back in no time! We need tuh make it on the porch—*quick*!"

"Remember! We've got to be *quiet* about this! We must *hurry!*" Lucy hissed.

"Yuh *ready,* Angus?" Ellie whispered, as she crouched low.

Angus nodded. He was ready for what they had planned.

Ellie stretched out on the ground.

The little wet dog climbed on her back. He tucked his paws under her leather collar.

Ellie walked up the steps as Angus held on tight. She stopped when she reached the gate. She hung her large head over it with Angus on her shoulders.

Lucy jumped onto the porch rail. "*Holly!*" she whispered. "Drag your *blanket* over here! Angus will have a *softer landing* that way!"

Holly pulled her blanket to the gate and nudged it into an untidy pile with her nose.

Angus looked around Ellie's huge head to see just where it was that he was supposed to land.

Ellie stood steady as Angus balanced himself on her head.

"Okay, Angus! Remember! On *three!*" Lucy hissed.

"Okay," Angus said.

"'You ready, Ellie?" Lucy asked the big dog.

Ellie wagged her tail and waited for Lucy to give the signal.

Lucy said, "*One!*"

Angus' heart was beating fast.

"*Two-o-o—!*"

Ellie took in a slow deep breath, and closed her eyes.

"*Three!*"

Ellie thrust her head forward! Right down the front of her big, wooly face, Angus went!

He landed dead-center.

"*Bingo!*" Lucy whispered.

"*That's* the way, young'in!" Cap chuckled.

"Dry yourself!" Holly whispered. "*Hurry*, Dear!"

Everyone watched as the pup wriggled and squirmed in the soft fleece, drying himself all over.

Holly smiled and licked the pup's sweet face. "Oh! *Angus!* I'm so glad you're *home!*" she cried.

Lass had run way past the shed, with Mike and Kate right behind her.

"C'mon, Lass! *Stop!* That's *enough* now!" Kate called out to her baby.

Bill Dawson had seated himself on the back porch step. He was chewing a toothpick, waiting for them to return with that little ol' fast runner!

Lucy looked at Cap and said, "Ok, Cap! Now *you!*"

Holly and Angus sat side by side, watching Cap as he climbed onto the big dog's back.

Ellie started up the steps once more.

Cap made his way to the top of her head.

"Okay, Cap. On *three*," Lucy whispered.

Cap nodded.

"One! Two! *Three!*"

Cap landed squarely onto the blanket.

"*Bull's eye!*" Lucy said, with a twitch of her tail.

Cap got to his feet and shook his fur.

"'Glad you're *home*, Cap!" Holly said, beaming.

"*Aye, Lassie*! We'r-rre glad-d tooo *be* home!" he replied, through his wide, whiskery smile.

Lucy jumped down from the porch rail. "I'll be *back*! I need to talk to Judy and Rex. I need to let them know that everything's al*right*!"

"They're waitin' tuh heer," Ellie said, as she settled onto the step.

Lucy bounded toward the barn.

"What doo we doo about *Lass*?" Cap asked, knowing that she'd be caught soon.

"We'll just let them think she got *loose*!" Holly exclaimed, happy with her idea.

"Alrr-rright! That's what we'll *doo*!" Cap agreed.

Ellie thought for a minute. "Yup. That shud work," she said.

Angus hung his head. He didn't want Lass to be in trouble because of what he had done.

Ellie knew how bad he felt. "Aw, she won't be in too much of a fix, Angus. I'm tellin' yuh. It'll be okay."

"Ellie's *right*, Dear," Holly said.

"It will be all *well and good*, young'in," Cap chimed in.

"I got tuh do rounds. I'll check in with yuh in a short while," Ellie said softly. She nuzzled the pup with her nose.

Holly grabbed her blanket. She dragged it back to its place by the wicker chair.

It was just a moment or two later that The Stranger climbed the steps. He looked over the gate.

Holly studied him.

"*Hey, there*! Well, aren't you a bunch o' *dandies*!" the cheerful voice said.

100

"*Don't moove, young'in,*" Cap whispered to Angus.

Ellie stood silently in the shadows, her eyes focused upon the man.

"Ellie! Come!" Mike said from behind them. "That's *Bill*! He's a *friend* of mine!"

Bill spun around as the Airedale trotted to her master.

"How you doin', Ellie? *Huh?*" Mike said, tousling her whiskers.

Ellie wagged her tail.

"*Whew!* I'm glad *you're* here! I was just lookin' at these little ones here on the porch. Why, I didn't know that that *big dog* was anywheres close by!"

"Yeah, well, that's how she *is*—a good *farm* dog! I don't have to worry about a *thing* with *her* around!" Mike bragged.

Kate came around the corner with a smiling Lass.

"Hi, *loves! Oh!* I'm so glad you didn't get *loose too,* Sweethearts!" Kate said, as she fussed with her girl—setting her down gently inside the gate.

"*Mike*! We're going to have to look this porch **over**, and figure out how it is that she got **out**! I'm so grateful that none of the others *followed* her!" Kate gasped.

"I'll take a good look in the mornin', hon."

Kate smiled at her loves there, all in a row—Holly, Cap, Angus, and Lass. She turned to Bill. "These are my little ones, my *babies*. I treat them as if they're *human* sometimes, I suppose," she said, nearly blushing.

"Yes ma'am. They sure are cute!" he said.

"This is *Holly*, and this one's *Cap*, and this is *Angus*," Kate said, pointing to each one. She laughed. "And you've already *met* Lass!"

Bill chuckled. "Yes ma'am!"

"Well, if you'll excuse me, I need to get them fed," Kate said. "They're hungry, I'm sure! Mike, I'll feed Ellie too. I know you have things you need to get done so that we can all get to bed."

"Thanks, hon. That'll be great. Bill, you wanna do a few rounds with me an' Ellie here? You're welcome to take a look at the place."

"I'd sure like to, but it's gettin' late. Sarah's probably frettin' about why I ain't home by now. Maybe next time?"

"I understand. Some other time," Mike said.

Bill looked at Kate. "It was nice meetin' ya, Ma'am."

"Bill, it was so nice meeting you too—and Sarah! I had a *lovely* day!"

"You and Sarah will be in touch?" he asked.

"Yes, of course!" she said. "I'll call her tomorrow."

He reached out and shook her hand. "Talk to you again soon, Ma'am. Have a good evenin'."

"Thank you. Oh, *Mike*? Would you mind letting them off the porch for a minute while I fix their supper?"

"Sure. I'll do that," Mike said.

Kate started for the kitchen.

Mike unlatched the gate and the four terriers bounced down the steps.

Bill patted Cap on the head as he went by. "They sure are *somethin'*!" he said.

"Yeah, *Kate* sure enjoys them! Well—*I* do too," Mike confessed.

Kate remembered the laundry that was hanging on the line but no longer worried about it. It would wait until morning.

She picked up Ellie's dinner bowl off the back porch and washed it in the sink.

She went into the utility room and took the other four bowls from the shelf. She scooped dry food into each one, making sure that Angus and Ellie had more than enough.

Kate opened the refrigerator and looked for something good to add to their meal. She took the small bowl of beef gravy from the shelf and grabbed the left-over biscuits. She thought for a moment. She remembered the small dish of peas and carrots that was there. (Cap loved carrots!) She took that bowl out too.

Kate broke the biscuits into pieces as the gravy and vegetables heated in a saucepan on the stove.

Holly's mouth watered. She could hear that her supper was almost ready!

Kate poured the warm mixture over the biscuits and dry food. She took a large wooden spoon from the drawer and stirred each meal.

"'Anything else?" she wondered. She took the jar of strawberry jelly from the table. She spooned a bit onto the side of each meal. She looked at Holly's dish. She gave her one more.

Kate picked up the largest bowl and carried it outside. She called Ellie.

The Airedale came running.

Kate returned to the kitchen as the big dog sprang to the porch.

Ellie sniffed her bowl. Instantly, she began gulping.

Mike stepped onto the porch as Bill Dawson got into his car and started the engine.

Ellie paid no attention to her new friend's leaving. Her front feet were planted firmly on either side of that stainless steel bowl and her head was well into it.

Bill turned his car around. He waved one last time to Mike as he stepped on the gas.

Mike walked toward the barn.

Kate placed each dish on the floor in the utility room in its usual spot—Holly and Cap's to the far left—Lass' dish near the clothes basket—and Angus' bowl just inside the doorway.

The four dogs focused their eyes upon the front door as Kate came for them. "Al*right*! It's *ready*, loves! *Suppertime*!" Kate happily announced.

Angus led the way, with Cap and Holly right behind. Lass shook herself and walked a short distance apart.

Holly nosed her bowl and lapped the sweet jelly first.

Cap sniffed and chewed each bite of his meal. He could not help but notice how wonderful those carrot bits, those sweet, juicy, *delightful*, carrot bits tasted—all coated with that warm, *beefy* gravy!

Angus devoured his food, scooting his bowl across the concrete floor as he ate.

The scraping sound that the metal bowl made was a sound that the others were quite used to.

The bowl finally came to a stopping place near the washing machine.

Angus licked the smooth metal—hoping to find one more taste of something—one more taste of *anything*.

Lass still had half of her dinner in her dish.

Angus eyed her bowl.

Lass sniffed and decided that, *yes*, she *would* eat her strawberry jam tonight!

Angus watched her as she lapped at the small mound.

Lass smoothed her whiskers with her tongue. She looked at the pup. "Angus, I'm *full* now. If you'd like the rest of *mine*, you may *have* it."

Angus cocked his head. "*Really*?" he said.

"*Yes*," she replied, sure of it.

The pup walked straight to the bowl and began gulping.

Holly walked to the kitchen. She watched as her Mimi put the last of the canned goods into the pantry.

"Hi there, Sweetheart! Did you have a good *supper*?" Kate asked her.

Holly wagged her tail.

Cap and Lass came into the kitchen and sat.

Kate smiled. "Well! I guess *everyone's* had a *good supper!*" she said.

Lass smoothed her whiskers with her long, pink tongue.

Kate took a second look. She now saw that someone was missing. "Where's *Angus*?" she asked them.

Her babies looked at her, adoringly.

Kate walked to the wash room. Holly, Cap, and Lass followed right behind. She stopped in the doorway. *"Aww—"* she whispered to herself.

Holly sighed.

Cap's eyes twinkled.

Lass looked too, with loving eyes.

There he was, sleeping next to Lass' dish.

Kate picked him up in her motherly hands.

His brown eyes opened slightly as she gave him a gentle kiss on the head.

Kate placed him in his soft, warm bed. *"Good night, Angus,"* she whispered.

He closed his eyes again, and dreamed of home.

Kate took up the feeding dishes and walked toward the back porch.

Holly, Cap, and Lass followed, but she made them stop when she reached the back door. *"Stay*, loves," she said.

She placed the four bowls outside on the porch next to Ellie's. She'd wash them in the morning after breakfast.

"Okay. 'Time for bed, loves," she whispered to her babies.

Cap walked straight to his bed and snuggled down into it.

Holly turned around twice and nestled herself into her own cozy place.

Lass did not go to her bed. Instead, she curled herself around on the floor — next to Angus.

"*C'mon, Lass.* Go to your *bed*, love," Kate said with a sigh.

Lass looked at Kate sheepishly, but she did not move.

"*Alright,*" Kate said softly. "If you want to sleep *there*, then *go ahead.*"

Lass closed her eyes.

Kate turned off the light and walked to the back door. She looked out. She wondered if Ellie was with Mike. She was sure that she was.

She yawned and walked to the bedroom.

No one saw Ellie as she peeked from behind the sofa. She had been hiding there — waiting.

The big dog's usual place for sleeping was outside in her dog house — but not tonight.

Ellie walked quietly through the kitchen.

She poked her head around the half-opened door and looked at them — her friends — sleeping peacefully.

Her eyes searched for a place to lie down. She chose a spot near Cap.

The big dog rested her chin on her paws and closed her eyes.

She was glad to be home.

Part Seven

~ Lessons Learned ~

Mike had awakened early. He moved quietly through the house. Kate was still sleeping.

Ellie crept out of the washroom and nudged the screen door open. She lapped a cool drink from her water bucket and started off.

Mike walked the perimeter of the porch. He did not see any loose or missing slats. He checked a second time, wondering how it was that Lass could have gotten out.

He picked up his coffee and took a sip.

Kate came outside with two cinnamon rolls — the store-bought kind.

"Good morning! Did you sleep well?" Mike asked.

"Good morning! Yes! I did!"

Mike took a bite of roll. He talked and chewed at the same time. "I didn't find any bad places in the rail, Kate. I checked it twice."

"Then, you're *sure*?"

"Yeah," he said, still chewing.

"Well, she must have gone *over* the gate then?" Kate asked, somewhat surprised by the thought of it.

"Maybe. In any case, I'll add another board across the top of the gate this mornin'. I don't want you worryin' about them. *That'll* keep that front porch bunch in!" he said with a wink.

"Thanks, Sweetheart!" Kate said, quite relieved.

"I'm gonna call Don's garage this mornin' too, and see if they got the truck there okay."

Holly barked from inside the house.

Kate set her cup on the crate. "Guess they need to go *out!*"

"'Sounds like they *do*," Mike said.

Kate walked to the laundry room, where they were anxiously waiting for her. "Good morning, *loves*! *C'mon*! Let's go *outside!*"

The dogs followed happily, one after the other.

Kate opened the front door and let the dogs onto the porch. She unlatched the gate. They scampered down the front steps and into the yard.

Mike frowned at the gate. "I'll give that gate a fresh coat of paint today too, while I'm at it. It's getting pretty *scratched up* I see —"

"Yes. It's been like that for quite a while now," Kate confessed. "Well, *dogs will be dogs!*"

"*Sure*," Mike had to admit.

"Stay *close*, now!" Kate called to her babies.

Angus looked at Cap. "'No more runnin' off for *me!*" he whispered.

"*Aye?* Yoo lear-r-rned your-r-rr *lesson* then, did yoo, Laddie?" Cap asked.

"You bet I did!" Angus said. "No more *explorin'* for *me!* Not unless *Katie and Mike* are there!"

"*Good for-r yoo,* young'in!" Cap said, flashing a smile.

He peered at the pup. "So, *tell me then.* What *else* did yoo lear-r-rn?"

Angus looked Cap straight in the eye. "Well, I learned that I need to be *good!* I need to not ever make Katie and Mike *worry!* I need to *follow the rules,* 'cause they keep me *safe!*"

"*Aye!* They *doo!*" Cap agreed.

"*Cap?*"

"Yes, young'in?"

"I have the *best* friends in the *whole world!*"

"Doo yoo *think* so?" Cap chuckled.

"*Yeah!* You guys didn't stop lookin' for me! You *found* me!"

"Well, good fr-r-riends ar-re *har-r-r-rd* to come by!" Cap acknowledged.

"And I learned somethin' else, *too!*" Angus said.

"*What's that?*"

"*Katie* and *Mike?* They woulda been *so worried* if they knew what I did!"

"*Aye!* They would have *been!*" Cap said.

Angus lowered his head. "Katie woulda *cried,* I bet."

Cap spoke gently. "Young'in, we all know that yoo'r-re sor-rry for-r what yoo did. And, yoo say that yoo won't doo it again? *R-rright?*"

"*Yeah.* I won't *ever* do that again. I *promise!*" Angus said.

"Well, then it's behind us now, Laddie," Cap said softly, smiling at the pup.

Angus smiled back. He knew that Cap was right this time.

Ellie carried her tire to the corner of the house. She dropped it on the ground and barked at Mike, wanting him to play.

"Not *this early*, Girl!" Mike told her. "I'll throw it for ya later, *okay*? I've gotta finish my *breakfast* first!"

Ellie wagged her tail and barked again.

Mike grinned at the dog. "No. In a little while, I said."

Ellie picked up her tire and walked toward the back yard as a bird's song filled the morning air.

Lucy sat on the fence near the barn. She looked at the farmhouse and mewed.

"*Cap?*" Angus asked.

"*Aye?*"

"*Lucy?*" he said, glancing at the cat. "I used to not *like* her—but now I *understand*."

"'Under-rr-rstand *what*, young'in?"

"Well, we never gave her a *chance*. We never gave her the chance to be our *friend*."

"That's *tr-rr-rue*, young'in. We *didn't*," Cap agreed.

"And look at how it all turned out!" the pup said.

"'Looks like we *all* lear-rr-rned a lesson yester-r-rday, Laddie!" Cap said.

Lucy mewed again.

Cap yipped cheerfully to her.

Lucy smiled—a genuine, friendly smile.

Mike whistled. "C'mon, Girl! 'Wanna help me cut some *boards*? I promised *Kate* that we *would*!"

The Airedale came running and joined him at his left side.

"Well? Let's *go*! We'd better get down to the *shed*! We got a lotta work to do today, Girl. 'Ya *ready*?"

"**Woof**!" Ellie said.

"C'mon, Sweethearts!" Kate said. "Not too *far* now!"

Holly and Cap scampered toward Kate, with Lass and Little Angus not far behind.

"*Angus*?" Lass said.

"*Yeah*?"

"*'Wanna play a* **game** *with me*?"

"*Sure*!"

"*Okay*," Lass giggled. "*You're* **IT**!"

Printed in the United States
74236LV00006B/289-384